FORSAKING THE FIFTH

Casey Jo Jukes

ISBN-13: 978-0692392485 (Casey Jo Jukes)
ISBN-10: 0692392483

DEDICATION

IN LOVING MEMORY OF FRANCES BEALE RAMSEY,
"AUNT FRAN."
A DEAR AND WONDERFUL LADY!

ACKNOWLEDGMENTS

I am extremely grateful to my friend and editor, Linda Sisneros, for her diligent efforts in polishing and honing this story. Our extensive discussions have continually helped to clarify and refine the conceptual ideas for this manuscript.

I give special thanks to Spencer Bancroft for his technical assistance with the cover design. My continued gratitude to my husband and family for their love, support, and patience. I love you!

DISCLAIMER

This is a work of fiction. All characters appearing in this work are fictitious. Any resemblance to real persons, living or dead, is purely coincidental. All names, locales, and incidents are products of the author's imagination or used fictitiously.

"ROADHEADER" excavation equipment

This piece of heavy equipment (a roadheader) is used to excavate tunnels. I have utilized a roadheader within the *course* of this novel. Therefore, I've included this picture to help you, the Reader, conceptualize the 'machine.'

PROLOGUE

Alone. Elizabeth sat in the ebbing light of dusk, watching the subtly shifting shadows of the encroaching darkness. Only the low hum of the television offset the quiet of this room. The stillness was unnerving. Her friends had gone camping at the river, but she had begged off because she didn't want them to see her so wacked out. Besides, she had college applications to fill out; which had been a lame excuse to her friends for not joining them. To start, she only needed to fill out the financial aid application for college tuition, and apply for housing in the dorms. So easy, why was she just sitting here, doing absolutely nothing? But she knew the answer!

For three weeks, she'd been couch surfing; going from one friend's house to the next. She was trying to figure out her next, best, move to get on with her life. The money she'd saved for startup costs wouldn't last long if she didn't get started -doing something. Somehow, she could not get her mind sufficiently wrapped around her future when it was so firmly embedded in the past. How could she move on when her sister, Tabitha, was still out there lost. .... "Or was she?" Elizabeth acknowledged with a sting, intensifying her misery.

She replayed the recorded video segment of the newsmagazine, "*Mystery Source*," for the umpteenth time. Why was she watching this stupid piece over and over and over, again? She couldn't gain any clearer understanding from the minute scraps of information given. A serial killer, Eric Morrison, had murdered four young girls in Calaveras County from 1989, until his arrest in 1998. Each child was six or seven years old at the time of their abduction. Four bodies were found, but the authorities suspected there had been another victim. ...What the hell! What made the cops so damn sure there had been a fifth victim? There had been nothing in that report to even suggest there were any more victims. Maybe the cops were just full of shit! That wouldn't be the first time in her experience. Yet, the haunting question stealthily hovered in her mind. Could Tabitha have been the fifth victim of that Creep?

The last place her sister, Tabitha had been seen was in Calaveras County; in what? 1992, was nearly ten years ago. God, if only they could get a straight answer from Evelyn but her aunt was as nutty as they come. Now strongly medicated, the Bitch refused to say anything at all; pretends she doesn't remember. Hell, Evelyn probably killed Tabitha herself. It wasn't a far stretch to imagine that Evelyn lost control and snapped. Evelyn did beat the crap out of Tabitha at that campground just before Tabitha was taken into protective custody in Calaveras. Mom did try to get the authorities to investigate Tabitha's disappearance six years ago. But, no one would listen to her or take her seriously because of her history of losing children to the system.

Suddenly coming to a quick but firm decision, Elizabeth got up to flip on the lights, turning off the video recorder and TV from the remote. Tomorrow, she would head to Calaveras County, and even sleep in her car if she had to. Calaveras County was her starting point; she needed to find out all she could about the disappearance of Tabitha. Meanwhile, Elizabeth would submit her financial aid packet. She hoped to have answers about her sister before college started in the fall. However, this was probably just wishful thinking on her part; because she realized that these answers were not going to be easy to uncover.

CHAPTER 1

It was a long eight-hour drive to Calaveras County! Elizabeth' mind wandered aimlessly over her muddied past making frequent pit stops along the way. She could never remember having a stable home with her Mom or her sisters. It seemed that they were always just staying at someone's house before being kicked out and having to find another place to stay. Over and again; this pattern was like a dull refrain. She didn't know her father. Hell, Mom probably can't give me his name. She seriously doubted that any of her brothers or sisters had the same father. Her family was absolutely nuts. Why had it all seemed so normal to her at the time?

Now in retrospect, Elizabeth realized how crazy everyone seemed; all the drama and chaos that surrounded her during that time in her life. Every adult she met had been arrested at one time or the other; never knew one who hadn't been. Everyone fled and scattered like birds if a cop or county car was seen. The physical brawls and screaming matches were just a routine. Like the time Mom got into a fist fight with another woman. Mom really messed up the woman's face. Elizabeth remembered watching the fight from behind the recliner. She had been so scared because she thought that the police were going to come and hurt her mom again. The time before, the cop had hit Mom with his stick while trying to force her hands behind her back so he could handcuff her.

There were some good times too. The best time was when they had lived in an abandoned warehouse for several months before being found out. The depot was uncomfortable with the hard, cold cement floors. But, it had been so calm because there was no one else there except Mom and her sisters. Then, the cops told Mom she had to go because she was trespassing.

Elizabeth's Mom had no one else to turn to, and couldn't find a place to stay. Mom also said she was in a world of hurt because the cops were looking for her. So they had started hitch-hiking across the country from Florida. It was November; Mom and all three girls; each of us bare-footed with our hair encased with lice, filthy as all get out. We were sleeping in parking lots and in drug infested basements with all kinds of strange men.

When they arrived in Las Vegas, Elizabeth remembered being dazzled by all the beautiful lights, which lit up the sky. Then, they descended into the dark tunnels beneath the city streets of Las Vegas. It was like entering the gates of Hell! There were all kinds of scary people, mumbling sometimes, even screaming to themselves. She was so cold, frightened, and extremely tired. However, she refused to sleep, forcing herself to remain awake or who knows what could happen. She had to protect Tabitha; it was her responsibility. Mom had passed out for she managed to score a bottle.   Elizabeth knew how she had managed to procure a bottle, but she couldn't even admit it to herself, even now. She'd heard the rustle of clothes and the grunting. She just knew her mom was going to get Aids or something. When Sammy, her brother got there, she had said as much to him; blurting out that Mom was going to die from aids, sooner or later. Sammy told her to shut the fuck up for she was too young to know about such things.

Mom had lost Serena, Sammy, and Daniel to the social workers in Florida, ten years prior. Sammy would have been about six at the time. At sixteen, Sammy kept running away from his foster homes and finding us. Don't know how he ever managed to track us down each time but he'd catch up with us along the way, even across several states. I swear he must have been a dog in his previous life; the way he tracked us all down.

When the police came, Danielle ran away like usual; she was always taking off. Initially, it was just me and Tabitha that went to live with Aunt Evelyn, but eventually the police found Danielle. She was sent to live with Evelyn too. Elizabeth knew that Sammy had told the social worker where to find Mom and us because she had overheard Sammy talking with the social worker that night. She had listened hard even though she had to pretend to be playing so they'd continue to talk in front of her. If they knew, she was listening they'd whisper and move away from the area. The adults had always done that.

The lady social worker told him that he had done the right thing by helping protect his little sisters. She also told him that Mom hadn't changed in the ten years since he went into care. If she hadn't changed in all that time, what made him think she ever would? In fact, it was highly unlikely that she ever would. Also, she was facing charges in Florida for Arson; she set something on fire for money so she'd be facing prison time. She told him he shouldn't run away anymore for it was only two years until he'd get out of the system and then, he could go wherever he wanted.

"What was Sammy thinking, that if the family all got back together, we'd be the Brady bunch or something?" That was the last time she'd seen her brother. Sammy was sent back to Florida that night on the plane. Maybe she could look him up and see if he's okay. She didn't even know Serena or Daniel. They had been placed in foster care before she was even born, but Sammy had told her all about them. Would any of them want a relationship with her at this point? Was she just chasing shadows, in hopes of finding something real and solid that she could hang onto? Maybe it was better to keep looking at her past through the rearview mirror and build something completely different out of her life.

Elizabeth shifted her position behind the wheel; she needed to find a rest stop soon. A cup of coffee would do her good. Her mind quickly dived back into the past again. She and Tabitha had been placed in guardianship with their aunt and uncle, Evelyn and Wade Heald in Sheldon, CA   Later, when Danielle was found, she was sent to live with Aunt Evelyn too. Somebody should have had a clue that it would be a disaster from the get-go.

She had never even met her aunt and uncle before being placed in their home.   Evelyn and Wade had never had any children of their own. They did not want to be saddled with three children and then deal with all their problems.

And boy, there were problems from the very beginning.

Danielle was always taking off and running away. Her older sister never looked out for anybody but herself, and that had never changed. She constantly started problems or fights and then, she'd just disappear. She was never around to face the consequences or pick up any of the pieces after a blowout. "I always got stuck cleaning up her messes!"

Then, there was Tabitha. She did not talk, never uttered a word; she was diagnosed with selective mutism. I really don't know if Tabitha was unable to actually speak. Maybe by design, she chose to remain silent, in distain of the circumstances or in order to shut out the world. Ultimately, her little sister appeared ...well somehow, disconnected from the everyday matters. Aunt Evelyn would often say things that were unfair, mean-spirited, hurtful, or simply wrong; which Tabitha seemed unable to hear, understand. Maybe Tabitha just couldn't express her pain. Someone had to protect her because she couldn't defend herself. I guess that someone was me. As a result, I always seemed to be talking for both of us. In hind sight, I shouldn't have talked as much at the time but I couldn't help it. Talking always seemed to get me into all kinds of trouble. I always spoke what was on my mind, and didn't realize the kind of reception my words would get. Now thinking back, it was just the blunt honesty and candor of a six-year-old child.

However, Evelyn always took exception to what I had to say, as if we became locked in some invisible battle. Over the following months, I became the source of all Evelyn's problems and hang-ups; she could barely stand to look at me towards the end. Evelyn seemed to adore Tabitha because she never said anything and always just did as she was told. "Didn't Evelyn realize Tabitha never objected or talked back because she couldn't speak?"

"Hell, Evelyn even called me a thief and accused me of stealing." She found packages of Top Romen in my bed, and I got beat with a hair brush for it. I wasn't trying to steal anything! I was afraid that us- girls would go hungry again, when we left her house. I didn't quit taking the top Romen though, just learned to hide it better.

The relationship between my aunt and uncle became steadily

worse. Evelyn and Wade were always arguing and constantly at each other's throats. Sometimes, their arguments would turn into physical fights, mostly pushing and shoving matches. One morning after a long shouting match, Aunt Evelyn flung a bowl of cereal at Uncle Wade's head. "She hit her mark!" I can still remember the cereal and milk cascading down poor Wade's face.

One day, Danielle told a teacher that Uncle Wade had been making her touch him in the privates. The teacher told Danielle that she would have to tell the police about it. Again, Danielle took off and ran away before the police arrived at the school. I'm sure Danielle didn't want Evelyn to find out what she had revealed. "But then, I don't really know if Danielle was telling the truth or not. She was definitely a pro when it came to starting trouble!" The police came out to talk to Wade. But, Danielle had disappeared so no one could talk to her about it. Therefore, Uncle Wade wasn't arrested. He left the house and refused to come back.

From that time forward, Evelyn was more crazy and mean. It seemed like I was always walking a fine line to stop Evelyn from going off on me. But it didn't matter. Evelyn told the social worker that she wouldn't have me living under her roof anymore; they had to move me to some other home. After a meeting at the CPS offices, she refused to take me back home with her and they took me away from my sister. "I lost Tabitha that day, never saw her again. It's all my fault! It was my job to protect Tabitha. It always had been and without me there, Tabitha was lost."

We were supposed to see each other at the courthouse, have a visit while the guardianship was ended. Evelyn never showed up. I remember when I found out Tabitha wasn't going to be there. I started staring at the ceiling, bawling my eyes out. The social worker went to use the phone across the room and my attorney headed into the other room. All kinds of people were surrounding me but keeping their distance; I was crying my eyes out in the middle of the room. I have never been so alone in my whole life.

It reminded me of the story that Sammy had told me about being taken by CPS. Our Mom had been fighting with her boyfriend; the guy held a knife to her neck so police placed him and Daniel in protective custody. He'd been playing next door with his friend when he was put into a weird car by a stranger. He was crying harder and harder, no one said anything to him. He struggled to look out the window of the car and could see his sister -Serena running after the car. She was crying and couldn't catch up with them. At the time, he thought he'd been kidnapped. Later Sammy was placed in some foster home and it was explained to him what had happened. "Don't these government people know what the kids go through? They really don't have a fucking clue!"

For me, after that day in the courthouse, it was a constant stream of foster placements. Always being moved from one house to the next, my bags were never really unpacked. Never quite adapting or somehow fitting in. Every year, or sometimes even more often than that, I had a new set of foster parents, new school, and a new set of friends. Someday, I will find a nice town, buy a house, and I plan to die in the same house. One day, I will stop moving for good. I just need to find out where and then I'll make my plan.

Nine hours later, Elizabeth arrived at a coffee shop in Calaveras County, exhausted from the long drive and her sojourn into the past. It always depressed her to think about what was "her childhood." She just wished she could wipe her memory clean. What would it be like to have amnesia and not have to remember your own history? If she got her memory back, would she reclaim her past? Stiffly, she got out of the car and stretched her muscles, and headed into the restaurant.

As the waitress seated her, Elizabeth hastily requested coffee before the waitress was out of earshot. In the adjacent booth, a family group was seated. It looked like a husband and wife with their little girl and a single guy in his early twenties. She checked him out for he was rather cute, he had dark wavy hair and grey eyes. The waitress came back and she ordered a BLT with fries. Now, the little girl was peeking over the back of the seat, watching her. Elizabeth's food arrived a short time later and Elizabeth started to eat. The little girl in the next booth was playing with her infant cup against the back headrest. Suddenly the cup top came off, splashing water across the seats, rivets of water streamed and pooled against Elizabeth's pants soaking her pant leg. Abruptly, she stood up to avoid the spill.

"Kayla!" the mother said in a raised voice, as she stood up. The little girl burst into tears.

"It's alright, just a small spill," Elizabeth responded instinctively.

"I'm so sorry." The mother apologized. "Let us pay for your dinner."

"No, really it's okay." Elizabeth said. The young man that Elizabeth noticed earlier, scooted out of the booth. He went to one of the tables in the central corridor and brought a chair back, placing it at the front of their booth. Then without a word, he picked up Elizabeth's plate and coffee cup and set it at their table. Elizabeth watched the quick movements, flabbergasted.

"By the time the mess gets cleaned up, your food will be cold. Come over and eat with us."

"Do I have a choice?" Elizabeth said half amused and half annoyed with his presumptiveness.

He grinned, "Not without looking peevish, angry, and rather impolite. I'm Klay by the way; this is my sister -Jean, her husband - John, and the little squirt is Kayla. I saw that you were sitting there alone, are you waiting for someone?"

"No. Thanks for inviting me over," she mused -lifting her eyebrows. "I'm Elizabeth," she said offering her hand to him and then, the rest of the group. Kayla was rubbing her eyes, peering out at her. "Hi Kayla, it's nice to meet you." Elizabeth was rewarded with a shy little smile.

Just as they were getting seated, the food for the table arrived. The waitress glanced at the unexpected guest at the table. Klay offered, "There was a small mishap and water was spilled all over the seat in that booth," he said pointing to the next table. "Sorry about the mess."

"We'll get it cleaned up." The waitress nodded as she distributed the plates and left the table.

"She was a good sport about it; didn't even look annoyed. We'll have to leave her a good tip, won't we John?" Klay said congenially. They made small talk throughout the meal. Elizabeth remained mostly quiet, listening to their conversation. Kayla moved towards Elizabeth, and about half-way through the meal, sat on her lap.

"Kayla," Jean abolished. "My daughter sure does like you, she usually shyer than this."

"It's okay, she's not bothering me. I like little kids," Elizabeth said with a smile.

Elizabeth told the group that she was just traveling through town. Tomorrow, she was going to look up some family she had in the area, and asked about any reasonably priced, nearby motel. John gave her the name of a local motel and drew directions to it on a napkin.

At the end of the meal, John grabbed her bill. "No, let me get this; it's the least we can do."

"Thanks, it's awful nice of you. It was great meeting you, all." Elizabeth said, making her exit.

Elizabeth was dead on her feet, when she arrived at the motel. The place seemed safe enough and in a decent part of town. All was quiet, but not the scary, unsettling kind of quiet. She checked in and drove around to her room. She always liked to stay at ground level; just in case, she had to get out quick or something. Elizabeth got out her overnight bag, sleeping bag, and pillow. She didn't want to sleep in someone else's bedding, she was funny that way. Having her own sleeping bag and pillow, made her feel at home, safe, in some way. She'd learned it was good to keep a bag with all the essentials and a change of clothes, ever ready in her trunk. She had all her worldly possessions jammed in the back seat of her car, not much to speak of.

Anxiously, Elizabeth hoped she would be able to sleep once she got to bed. She was tense about going into the social services office tomorrow. She dreaded that place and promised herself never again, but she had to start somewhere. They couldn't keep her there now, so she had nothing to fear. Only bad memories and at least these memories couldn't hurt her.

Elizabeth knew she'd better call her friend, Ashley. The guys would be back from their camping trip now. Elizabeth had left a note, but she also knew that Ashley was going to be upset with her for leaving without talking it through with her first. Ashley knew her stay was only temporary, maybe she'd go back if she ran into a dead end here in Calaveras County regarding Tabitha. Elizabeth knew Ashley wanted her to get a job and stay on with her at the apartment, but that was not her plan at this time. She was going to find Tabitha and then start college somewhere. Maybe in the meantime, she could find a temporary job.

Elizabeth was right. Ashley hadn't liked the fact that she left without even saying good-bye. Ashley said that she'd been used. Elizabeth explained that she had pressing matters that she needed to attend to before she could settle down. Their conversation had been stiff. Elizabeth would call back and try to make amends in a couple of days. Give her a chance to cool off a bit.

Elizabeth was dragging as she got up the next day feeling slightly punch-drunk. The long drive to Calaveras County had wiped her out. Then, her heated conversation with Ashley had taken its' toll on her. Elizabeth had a difficult time falling to sleep and when she did, vague shadows hovered in her mind. Now, she had to go to social services and the dread of it made her feel teary. God, she despised that place.

Elizabeth dressed more formal than usual because she wanted the social worker to treat her like an adult and not view her as a child. She had to get her confidence up. She needed the social worker to get real with her and play it straight. She couldn't afford any excuses, detours, or lag time.

She fidgeted in the lobby waiting for the duty worker, rehearsing what to say. Assertive but not demanding; she couldn't afford to offend the social worker. Even with this thought, the sharp retorts and accusations filled her mind. How could they have let Evelyn get a hold of Tabitha after those people witnessed the beating, Evelyn gave her? They simply let Evelyn walk away with Tabitha! No! Elizabeth couldn't give this social worker a piece of her mind or this person may not help her.

The social worker came out and introduced herself as Nancy Taylor; she seemed nice enough. Then, Ms. Taylor directed Elizabeth to a small interview room. Elizabeth sat in the seat across from the lady and looked down at her tightly clenched hands. She started in, a little too rash and rushed. "C'mon chill." She thought.

"My name is Elizabeth Lenard. My Aunt and sister were traveling through this county when my sister -Tabitha was taken away from my Aunt by CPS, here in 1992. She was kidnapped or disappeared, but she hasn't been seen since...been missing for almost ten years. I'm trying to find out what happened to her."

"How can I assist you?"

"I'm trying to find my sister!" retorted Elizabeth flabbergasted.

"I'm sorry," said Nancy empathetically. "Listen, if your sister disappeared or was taken while in state's custody, there should be a police investigation. You may be able to find out more from the police. I'm not sure we would have any information to help you locate your sister, and besides, our records are confidential.

"She's my sister!"

"I know she's your sister. I'll tell you what, give me 15 minutes and I'll review what information we have, and I'll see if we have anything that will help you. Okay?"

"Okay," Elizabeth responded in frustration, as she watched the social worker exit the room. She hadn't been sure where this conversation would lead, but she hadn't expected this stonewalling.

"Chill!" She tried to loosen up, stretching and rubbing her tense muscles. The social worker wasn't gone long. Nancy Taylor sat down again across from her. "Elizabeth, I can't give you specific information due to the confidentiality of child welfare. Sad to say, there wasn't a lot of information in our report. What I can do is give you general information on how a social worker would approach an investigation and hypothetical concepts so you can piece together what happened. What do you know about what took place?

My aunt had left Tabitha alone at a campsite. As night fell, a family camping nearby told Tabitha to come inside their tent, for it was getting cold out. When Evelyn returned, she went ballistic because Tabitha had entered this family's tent. She pulled Tabitha out, screaming at her for being bad. The family saw Evelyn pin Tabitha down, bang her head into the ground, and slug her, several times. The police were called and Tabitha was placed in foster care. Later, Evelyn found out where the foster home was and took off with Tabitha.

Ms. Taylor responded, "When a social worker is called to the scene, they collect as much general information as they can about the reason a child is being placed in emergency care. They collect information about the child, and tell the parent or in this case, the guardian about the family court hearing on the matter. This hearing is to determine whether there is enough evidence to keep the child out of the care of the guardian. The guardian would also be cited for child abuse and ordered to appear on criminal charges. Sometimes the child is too emotional or traumatized to tell the police or social worker anything.

"My sister wouldn't talk; she had what the psychologist called, 'selective mutism.'" Elizabeth interrupted.

"The officers did not know why the child wouldn't speak and there weren't any significant visible injuries. The consensus of the police officers and the social worker would be to have the child examined at the hospital for any physical trauma. Hypothetically, the guardian might have overheard that the child was being taken to the hospital and grabbed the said child from the parking lot. Now, social workers are instructed not to engage with a parent or guardian taking off with a child because it can possibly escalate the danger. Therefore, a social worker would immediately call law enforcement and report the incident. Law enforcement would issue a nationwide alert for this person and child. Additional charges would be filed."

"If law enforcement was immediately notified. How did Evelyn get out of the area with Tabitha?"

Ms. Taylor shrugged, "Again hypothetically, there could have been a few complications, such as, an individual giving a phony identification and address to law enforcement. Moreover, this same individual could have given misleading information about the child to the authorities."

Elizabeth covered her eyes with the palms of her hand and said, "I get the picture. Evelyn showed up, homeless, living on the streets. They say she is psychotic; she is now hospitalized and on meds. Evelyn claims that she doesn't know where Tabitha is."

"I'm so sorry," Ms. Taylor responded.

Elizabeth hesitated, then fearfully continued. "I saw a newsmagazine program, 'Mystery Source,' it reported that a serial killer was targeting girls at the same age my sister was in the 1990's. The cops suspected that there were additional victims. Is there any way my sister could have been one of his victims?"

Ms. Taylor paused, "Your sister is still missing. From what you've told me, no one knows where she is or what happened to her after date of this incident. Maybe your aunt will give additional information if her mental health continues to stabilize. Hypothetically, the social worker saw who abducted this child and it would be the same woman that she saw earlier in the evening at the campsite. If that helps?

"What can I do?" Elizabeth pleaded.

"Just some general ideas: You could contact the Center for Missing and Exploited Children. Maybe they can put out a bulletin with a photo and an age progression photo, what your sister would look like today. They can also give you some good advice. You could talk to law enforcement to see if they ever got any leads on this case. Maybe even, this newsmagazine could do a segment on your sister?

"Thanks for talking to me," Elizabeth said hollowly, as she rose to leave.

Klay couldn't get Elizabeth off his mind, something intrigued him about her. He reminded himself that she was just passing through town, trying to locate family; then she would be gone. But somehow, this thought did not distract his thoughts away from her. Clearly, she was attractive in a fiercely independent way. He visualized her willowy figure with the long black hair and her amber eyes. She had strength and determination in her stance. However, it was more than just her looks that drew him to her. She was an enigma.

Last night, Elizabeth appreciated the company. However, he knew just as well that she would have refused the invite if he hadn't taken the initiative to bring her over to their table. And it wasn't just misplaced politeness or awkwardness that held her back. There was something desperately lonely about Elizabeth, yet she seemed completely comfortable with strangers. It was obvious that she was enamored with Kayla, couldn't take her eyes off the tot. Jean had said something about Elizabeth being reserved, but Klay didn't see it that way at all. He instinctively knew that she had a lot on her shoulders and was self-absorbed because of her difficulties.

He would go by the motel tomorrow with some funny ploy and try to strike up a conversation with Elizabeth. Would she accuse him of being pushy? He would have to think of a way to finesse her without getting on her nerves. He'd get to the bottom of what was going on.

Elizabeth arrived back at the motel. What in the hell had she gained by coming here? What a waste of time! She could have contacted the Center for Missing and Exploited Children from Sheldon. Had she thought that somehow her being in Calaveras County and this being the last place Tabitha was seen, would magically bring her closer to her sister? She really was too old for magical thinking; she needed to grow up already and face reality. The harsh reality is that is much more than likely that her sister was killed, over ten years ago or why hadn't she surfaced in all this time? Half determined to pack her things and hit the road, Elizabeth knew she just couldn't. She might as well finish the business, she set out to do. Next, she would contact the police and see if they had any additional information for her. While she was at it, she could contact the Center for missing Children from here. Might as well get as much bang for the buck, since she was already here.

The phone rang and she reached to answer it. The hotel clerk told her she had a visitor. Ms. Taylor wouldn't come to the motel; she couldn't have any more information. Could she have called the police to have them contact her? She got up and headed out the door towards the main lobby. Elizabeth saw Klay, as she approached. He turned and held out a small towel draped over his arm, formal like a maitre. "I come baring a peace offering for my boorish behavior last night, and as an apology for the unfortunate mishap that disrupted your quiet dinner. Will you accept my humble offering?"

Elizabeth laughed as she grabbed the towel to swat him with it. He feigned, fighting off the attack.

"Would you like to grab a cup of coffee with me? There's a coffee shop across the way."

"I could use a cup of coffee, right about now. Thanks."

They walked across the street and were promptly seated. Klay said, "Coffee for me," and glanced in her direction.

"Same here and could we get some cream." Elizabeth said as the waitress nodded and moved off.

"How's the search for your family members going?" Klay asked.

"Slow, they may not be in this area after all," Elizabeth responded.

"Well, let me know if there's any way I can help," Klay offered.

"I don't think there's any way you can help, but thanks all the same. What kind of work do you do, Klay? "Elizabeth said swiftly, changing the subject.

"I'm doing a paid internship at the College, and finishing my last year before I get by Bachelor's degree in Engineering.

"Where are you going to school?" She asked.

"Acadia College, it's about 45 minutes from here. I'm on summer break. What about you?"

"I'm between jobs right now. I may start college this fall, but I'm not sure yet." At his direct look, she continued. "I was in the foster care system. For the last two years, I lived in their transitional housing apartments while I finished high school and worked part-time. I completed some of the basic college courses. I should be able to start as a sophomore if I can transfer all my courses. I saved a little bit and want to see if I could locate some family members before I commit to college."

"I see. I could just tell you had a lot on your mind, when we met last night. Again the offer of help stands, my Dad knows a lot of people in the community. He might be able to put you on the right track."

"I'll keep your offer in mind, but you better give me your number in case I take you up on it."

"You bet," Klay said grinning.

After their coffee, Klay walked Elizabeth back to the motel. Arriving at the front lobby, Klay said, "at the risk of being too forward, how about having dinner with me tonight?"

"Taking pity on the lonely stranger in town?" She mocked.

"No, I find you irresistible. I could pick you up around six."

"Sounds like a plan, whatever will I wear?" she smiled.

"Whatever you feel like. There's a great steakhouse not too far from here."

"You're on, see you later;" she waved as she headed towards her room.

Elizabeth wondered what her next step should be. Should she contact the cops or the Center for Missing and Exploited children? On private matters, it was always easier for her to talk to a person rather than by phone or in writing. She could gauge their reaction so she would start at the police station. She found the address and located the address on the map in the phone book. She grabbed a notebook and pen along with an envelope, which held three photos of Tabitha, the only photos of her sister that she had.

She had waited over 45 minutes before she was able to meet with Officer James Crawford. Officer Crawford was in his early thirties with a solid build. He didn't seem intimidating. Again, Elizabeth checked herself, she was still guarded when it came to people "within the system." She tended to view "the authorities" suspiciously. "Remember, you need his help," she thought. He offered her a seat, before taking his own. Elizabeth sat stiffly in her seat, staring intensely at him.

"Umm ...how can I help you?" He looked uncertainly at her, taking in her defensive posture.

"I want to find my sister!" Elizabeth blurted out.

"She's missing?" He gently encouraged.

"Tabitha has been missing for almost ten years." Easy does it, she took a deep breath and continued. "She was taken away from my aunt, who had guardianship of her by the police. On the same night, she was kidnapped from the hospital and hasn't been seen since. Tabitha was 6 years old at the time. .....I was told a couple of years ago that my aunt was found living in a homeless shelter, and she says she doesn't know what happened to Tabitha!"

"I see," he replied solemnly. "I can look into the case history to see if we have any additional information," he shrugged his shoulders. "Missing persons cases are difficult; we are often left just waiting for new leads, and sometimes we don't get them. I can put you in touch with someone from the National Center for Missing and Exploited Children (NCMEC)."

"I looked up my sister's picture on the computer; it's an old one. You know, when she was six. I saw photos of other kids, which showed what they'd look like when they were older. How would I get one of those pictures? So it could be sent out."

"You mean an age-progression. The NCMEC could produce and distribute one, but I'll request it for you. The agency will produce one free for law enforcement."

"How long will it take?" Elizabeth asked impatiently.

"My guess, probably a week or two, but it will go out nationally." He responded, unconsciously scratching his head.

"I've got a couple of pictures of Tabitha for you, but I want them back."

"I can have copies made, and then, return them. Tell you what, leave your pictures with me. I'll review your sister's file, make copies of your pictures, and request that age-progression photo. Could you come back on Wednesday, and I will give you an update?"

"Okay," Elizabeth said, tentatively handing over the pictures. "What time?"

"Would two o'clock work for you?" Elizabeth nodded as she rose to leave.

"Uh....thanks," she fumbled.

"Okay, Wednesday then," Officer Crawford said, opening the door for her.

Elizabeth finished getting ready for her date with Klay, her almond brown eyes intently studying her reflection in the mirror. Her straight dark black hair swept the top of her shoulders, framing her oval face. She wore very little make-up, preferring a more natural look. The foundation hardly covered the freckles splattered across the bridge of her nose.   The light linen dress in a slight floral pattern fell just past her knees as she smoothed the dress down.

She was looking forward to having company for dinner but should she really have accepted the date? Klay seemed like a nice enough guy, but she needed to focus on finding Tabitha and getting everything ready to start school in the fall. Well, it was just a date for God's sake, not any sort of relationship. She knew what she wanted from life and exactly where she was going. She didn't need, want, or have time for a boyfriend in the mix. Klay would take her mind off Tabitha for a little while tonight.

Grimacing, she reminded herself to ask Klay if he knew of any room that she could rent for a month or two. It was going to take some time to find Tabitha and her money would not hold out if she were paying for a motel room. She grabbed her keys and purse as she headed out the door to the lobby.

Klay was already there, waiting for her. He looked attractive in his jeans and button up shirt as he held open the door for her. "Am I running late?" Elizabeth inquired.

"I'm a little bit early, you look nice." He complimented.

"Thanks. We could walk to the restaurant if it isn't too far. It's a nice evening."

"Sounds good to me," Klay replied.

The walk was nice and pleasant; the conversation light, as they arrived. The "Longhorn Smokey Grill" was an eye-catching, western-style restaurant, set deep off the main road. The restaurant had creamy yellow exterior with western themed accent pieces such as an old buckboard wagon, off to the side of the building. The steakhouse also hosted an adjacent brick courtyard for outdoor dining.

"Would you like to eat indoors or outside on the patio?" Klay inquired as they entered the front entryway.

"The patio would be nice," Elizabeth replied.

The hostess took Klay's name and told him there would be a fifteen-minute wait for patio seating.

Elizabeth sat down with Klay, taking in the interior of the restaurant. It had a nice atmosphere. There were some gumball machines and a "prize grabber" arcade game at the end of a small enclave. Klay stood up and fished through his pockets, grabbing some change.

"I used to be pretty good at those machines," Klay said as he headed toward the arcade game.

Elizabeth looked at him in surprise as he maneuvered the game controls. After a failed attempted, Klay managed to win a stuffed animal; which was a lavender elephant with a soft flowered pattern. He brought 'his win' back and placed it in Elizabeth's hands. Funny, Elizabeth could never remember receiving a stuffed animal as a gift before; she was touched by the gesture. A warmth filled her as she looked at the elephant, and then, shyly glanced up at Klay. "Thanks." She said throatily, holding up her gift.

The hostess came up to show them to their table on the patio. After they were seated, Elizabeth turned to Klay and said. "Klay, before I forget to ask. Do you know of any room I can rent for a month or so? Not too expensive."

"Well, I'd offer to share my place, but it's in Acadia."

"You are presumptuous and full of yourself! Aren't you?" She responded incredibly.

"A little, maybe," he offered with a grin. "I will ask around and let you know what I find." The waitress came over to take their order.

CHAPTER 2

Klay called the next day in the early afternoon. "Elizabeth, I think I've found a place for you to stay; the perfect set-up."

"Great! Tell me about it?"

"My sister -Jeannie has an older neighbor, Marion. This woman had a hip replacement surgery last week. She is recuperating at her sister's apartment in Acacia. She'll be convalescing for six weeks. Her daughter and son-in-law are taking care of Marion's house and dog while she's away. It hasn't been easy for Terri, her daughter, to take care of these responsibilities on a daily basis due to the time demands.

Jeannie suggested to Marion that you might be willing to house-sit while she is away. You could take care of the garden and her dog in lieu of rent. Marion was leery because she doesn't know you. But, Jeannie offered to oversee the situation and takeover if there were any problems. Marion agreed to the situation based on Jeannie's oversight if you are willing. What do you think?"

"It sounds like a great plan! Who do I talk to?" Elizabeth asked.

"I can meet you in front of your motel at five, and you can follow me to my sister's house. Jeannie will take you over and introduce you to Steve, Marion's son-in-law. He will give you the keys and the low down on what needs to be done.

"But Klay, can I leave the dog alone at the house when I have appointments?"

"Marion knows that you will be in and out of the house during your stay there. She told Jeannie that she leaves her dog, Ellie, in the screened-in patio area when she leaves the house. Marion has been worried about Ellie and in fact, she is relieved that her dog will be staying with you. Terri's fifteen year old made it to state on her high school volleyball team, so the family is hardly ever home with the dog. And her sister's apartment complex doesn't allow for pets." Klay concluded.

"Thanks, you're a life saver! I'll see you at five."

"See you then," Klay finished.

As she hung-up the phone, Elizabeth smiled, recalling the brief, tender kiss that Klay had given her last night. She had been apprehensive when he made his move; fearful that he would try to come onto her, way too fast. But, he was polite; he didn't attempt to press his advance any further. And now, he had found a safe place for her to stay, and it wasn't going to cost her anything. She was lucky to have met him when she did.

Jeannie was out on her porch when Klay, and then Elizabeth, drove up. She hustled over to greet them.

"Hi Elizabeth, I hate to rush you but Steve has to leave soon. I'll take you over to Marion's house, right now. Her house is the brick one, over there with the arched entry." Jeannie pointed to a house across the street and catty-corner to her own.

"It looks nice," Elizabeth replied as she and Jeannie started towards the residence.

"Steve has to get back to take care of his younger kids because Terri and her daughter are leaving town for a meet."

A slim guy, with dark brown hair was leaning against a work truck. He stood up straight as Elizabeth and Jeannie approached.

"Hi, I'm Elizabeth; you must be Steve," Elizabeth said as she held out her hand.

"It's good to meet you; I'll show you around the place." Jeannie stood back, allowing Steve to show Elizabeth around Marion's house and property, explaining what needed to be done before returning to his truck.

"Now, I'll get Ellie for you," Steve said, reaching through the door of the truck. He picked up a very small, delicate dog; it couldn't weigh more than seven pounds. She was pure black with silky, long hair. Steve sat the dog on the ground. Elizabeth knelt down beside her, and the dog proceeded to curl up into Elizabeth's arm, taking Elizabeth by surprise.

"You two will get along just fine," Jeannie remarked.

"I'd better get going," Steve said, handing Elizabeth a house key.

"Thanks, it's nice to meet you," waving as he drove off.

"I'll let you get your stuff unloaded and situated, Elizabeth. But then, c'mon over we're barbecuing some hamburgers."

"Thanks, that's good of you.

"It's great to have company for a change."

"Can I bring Ellie with me?"

"Yes! Of course, you can."

The next morning, Elizabeth awoke with a start. Where was she now? She looked around the quaint room and noted the abundance of framed family pictures throughout. Her bewildered gaze lingered on a few of the photos before it finally registered. Oh yeah, Marion's house, she recalled as Ellie moved from her dog bed onto the sleeping bag to snuggle with her.

Elizabeth got up and took Ellie outside to use the bathroom.

The backyard was neatly landscaped with comfortable patio furniture. She proceeded to water the grounds and garden as Ellie lapped along beside her. She soon finished her rounds. Her meeting with the cop, Crawford, was set for two o'clock. Not much to do until then, except find a grocery store and stock up. She could do with a cup of coffee. After filling the dog bowls with food and water, Elizabeth secured Ellie within the patio enclosure, and then went inside to get dressed.

She returned an hour later with groceries; she placed her provisions neatly on the counter and in the front portion of the refrigerator. Ellie was excited to see her. As Elizabeth led the dog into the house, the phone rang. Should she answer it? Yes, it could be Jeannie. She reached for the phone decidedly.

"Hello?"

"Hello, is this Elizabeth?"

"Yes, I'm Elizabeth."

"Good. I'm Marion. I wanted to call and find out if you settled in okay."

"Oh yes, thanks for letting me stay! Your house and yard are wonderful. And Ellie is great.

"I'm glad you like it. Do you have any concerns or questions about Ellie or the house?"

"No, not so far. Steve gave me a list of instructions and showed me around your place. I enjoy taking care of Ellie; I've never met a sweeter dog."

"I'm glad to hear it. I miss my baby. I'll give you my number here, in case you need it."

"Okay, let me grab a pen. ...Okay, what's the number?"

"It's 678-2354. I'll let you go," she concluded.

"Thanks for calling, I'm glad I have your number. Would you

like me to give you a call back in a couple days so I can give you an update?"

"That would be wonderful, dear. I'll talk to you later."

Elizabeth didn't have anything to do. She might as well take Ellie for a walk in the neighborhood to kill the boredom. As Elizabeth stepped outside, she saw Jeannie and Kayla heading quickly in her direction.

"Hi Elizabeth, I just wanted to check in with you and see how you're fairing. I hope you weren't uneasy, last night. It must feel weird staying in a strange house, all by yourself!"

Elizabeth was taken aback by her comment; it was all too familiar to her. "No, not really. I'm used to it; I've moved around a lot."

"Well, I won't keep you; I see you're heading out for a walk. But remember, I'm right across the street if you need anything."

"Thanks, I'll remember that." Okay, what could I possibly be scared of or need help with around here. This neighborhood is like Mayberry.

Elizabeth walked Ellie around the neighborhood; she contemplated Jeannie's concerns about her staying in a strange house. Sadly, staying in new places was commonplace for her. Elizabeth considered exactly how many foster homes she'd lived in throughout her childhood. How many strangers and weird environments had she adjusted to over those years? The social workers were always so nonchalant about moving her to a new placement. Why not? It wasn't like their lives were being turned inside out; their whole world was being torn apart. Each move meant: a new set of parents, a different family, along with changing expectations and rules. A change in friends; always being the 'new kid,' outside the social circle. And a different school, she lost so much in her schooling and education with each move. Her workers seemed to make these adjustments at the drop of a hat for their own convenience or ego demands. Didn't any of these people understand what it cost her, each time she was moved?

As Elizabeth drove towards the 'cop shop,' she willed herself to overcome her simmering frustration, which always gave way to open hostility, whenever she encountered 'the authorities.' But, these reactions seemed to be hardwired into her from an early age. She just didn't trust the cops. No one from her world did! As a kid, whenever she saw a cop, it meant trouble! Everyone was always being harassed by cops or running from them. There was that one night, when she saw the cop use the baton on her mom. Elizabeth knew that her mom was struggling to fight him off but beating Mom with that stick seemed a bit much. Then, she remembered that nasty bitch of a cop making crude, sarcastic comments about her mother when she and Tabitha visited Mom at the jail. The Bitch cop said things like her mom was a guest of the nowhere motel, where all little nobodies went. She'd even heard the woman refer to our family as 'dregs of society.' "I still can't believe she said mean things like that in front of me and Tabitha; we were just little kids!" Elizabeth could still feel the sting of her humiliation. She signed, maybe one day she would stop looking at the cops through the eyes of 'that' child.

"It's like being behind enemy lines," Elizabeth reflected as she entered the police station. Her palms were sweaty, her heart raced, her muscles ached from unrelenting strain, and she was alert to every sound or movement around her. As her alarm escalated, so did her throbbing headache. Elizabeth tried to quell her growing panic. Quietly, she asserted that she wasn't a "dependent ward of the court" anymore at "their" mercy or hapless prey to the foster care system. She yearned to cast away all remnants of "the system," including all the cops, social workers, and judges, associated with it.

Elizabeth informed the clerk that she had an appointment with Officer Crawford, and began her agitated wait. Thankfully, her wait wasn't very long this time; the cop came into the lobby and ushered her back. When Elizabeth entered the interior office, there was another "uniform" waiting there, with a grave expression.

"Elizabeth Lenard, this is Sheriff Neil Bryant; he would like to talk to you about your sister." Elizabeth had a sinking feeling in the pit of her stomach as she suspiciously eyed this unexpected visitor. The man held out his own hand, in order to shake hers' but Elizabeth failed to offer up her hand for the greeting. Instead, she backed away from this encounter.

"Ms. Lenard, here are your photos; I had copies made, and sent them to the NCMEC. You know the Center for Missing and Exploited Children. A technician is working on an age-progression photo; I'll give you an update when the photo is ready to send out nationally. Meanwhile, Sheriff Bryant has some additional information he would like to offer you regarding your sister's case. I'm going to leave and allow the two of you to discuss these developments." As Crawford took his leave, Elizabeth rationalized, the cops wouldn't have an age-progression photo authorized if they knew Tabitha was already dead. She sucked in air with some relief but still, she knew the pending information wasn't good.

"Ms. Lenard could you please have a seat." He said as he offered her a chair. She sat down, still on guard as he took his own seat.

"To start, I have spoken to both Officer Crawford and to Nancy Taylor from CPS. I was granted permission from the court to review the CPS file, and I've reviewed the police report regarding your sister's disappearance. I've also talked to the therapist, who is treating your aunt. I have a good understanding of what took place immediately before and after your sister's disappearance."

"What the hell is going on?" Elizabeth interrupted impatiently; this blow-by-blow accounting was agonizing.

"From what you told Ms. Taylor, you watched the episode 'involving the serial killer, Eric Morrison,' I initiated contact and closely worked with the *'Mystery Source'* producers of the show on that segment. My goal was to bring forth possible leads involving another possible victim. At the time, the killer was apprehended; my office had reason to believe there was possibly another additional victim unaccounted for. But, we had no information to pursue regarding the identity of this child. Last year, our department located an abandoned trailer, belonging to the killer. Within this trailer, we found photos of the (known) deceased children both before and after their deaths, along with other evidential materials. However, there was only one photo of a child that we couldn't identify. The child was alive when the photo was taken, and there were no subsequent death photos or other indicators of her death."

"It was Tabitha! That's why you're here," Elizabeth exclaimed.

"Yes, we believe it is a photo of your sister. The likeness is very similar to one of the pictures that you brought into the police station."

"But, the social worker indicated that my crazy...excuse me, my aunt, Evelyn Heald took off with Tabitha."

"Yes, from the police reports I've read and other statements given; your aunt absconded with Tabitha from the hospital parking lot. We simply don't know when, where, or how your sister became entangled with Eric Morrison. ...When we chose to air that episode with the newsmagazine, our hope was that this child escaped or somehow was returned to her family unharmed. Unfortunately, this was not the case."

"Why can't you make the killer tell you? The Creep knows what happened to her!"

Mr. Morrison isn't cooperating with law enforcement. He hasn't been forthcoming with any information regarding the child. I only wish I had more information to give you."

"How are you going to find out what happened to Tabitha? My sister has been missing for ten years!"

"First, I am confident that the girl within the picture is your sister. But, we want to make absolutely certain. Establishing the identity of the child is highly crucial. I have asked the FBI to compare the photos; the feds have highly advanced software. I would also like to take a DNA sample from you so we have a genetic sample on file for comparison purposes."

"What the hell am I supposed to do? Wait around until you find her body or you never find anything!" Elizabeth exploded.

"I need to level with you. I don't know what happened to your sister. She has been missing for a very long time. I don't want to hold out false hope that she is alive. However, I have no indications that she died at the hands of this killer. This perpetrator had a predilection for taking post-mortem photos. There were no death photos of this child discovered or other indicators of her death."

"Just fucking dandy! You still don't have a god-damn clue where my sister may be."

"I'm sincerely sorry about your sister. I understand how extremely difficult this must be for you. I trust that you will furnish a DNA sample. I will call you with an appointment time and give you updates as more information becomes available."

Elizabeth got abruptly to her feet without speaking, and made a rapid exit. She was going to lose it if she didn't get out of there quick. Her mind was racing, spinning uncontrollably. The anger, frustration along with the desperation, boiled to the surface, leaving her no outlet for this rampant upheaval. Her emotions, regarding Tabitha, had been held in check for too long -all these years, and now, she couldn't stem the flow. How could she cope?

She found a grassy, shaded area to sit down, trying to recoup. She never talked to anyone about her sister. It hurt too much! Nor had she completely accepted her secret fear that Tabitha was dead. Her sister was the only one that she was really close to. The only connection, which gave her a sense of family. Without Tabitha, Elizabeth had no one.

Should she call her Mom? Elizabeth didn't know how to define the relationship with her mother; except that it lacked any true depth or substance. It may be cruel to lay this abysmal situation out for her Mom. Tabitha was her youngest child after all, despite all the past problems. No, Elizabeth would deal with this situation on her own, and only call Mom, if she found out anything more concrete.

Elizabeth returned to Marion's house; only to pace around the place, driving herself crazy. Ellie maintained a constant vigil, staring at her with understanding eyes. The dog seemed to detect her mood, but knowingly maintained distance.

Elizabeth heard knocking at the door but failed to respond. The knocking continued unabated. She opened the door to find Klay standing there.

"Hello Elizabeth," Klay says with a grin. Then, he noted the look in her eyes and instantly sobered. "What's wrong?"

"Nothing, nothing; I'm fine. I don't want any company." Elizabeth said tersely, holding up her hands as to stop him from entering the house."

"You're not fine, Elizabeth. Could you please tell me what has happened?" He reasoned calmly.

"Listen, I told you that I want to be left alone. Just leave, get out of here!"

"Obviously, you're very upset about something and need to confide in someone. I take it that you're not in the mood to talk right now. I'll go back and sit in my car, and wait until you do want to speak. I can wait here all night if I need to;" he persisted as Elizabeth in answer, abruptly shut the door.

Klay was still seated in his car an hour later when Elizabeth looked out the window. The nerve of the guy! She'd just have to wait him out; he'd eventually get the hint. She went to feed the dog and straighten up the house. Another forty-five minutes had lapsed, and there was Klay still waiting out in the car. Finally, Elizabeth approached Klay.

"Listen Klay, I've had a rough day! I appreciate that you're only trying to help, but please just go home. I'm really not in the mood to talk about the problem right now.

"But, you will! Then, I'll leave."

"Ahh," Elizabeth let out a scream. "Damn-it! I don't want to talk about it."

"And I'm not leaving until you do. Have I told you that my main flaw is that I'm exceedingly stubborn."

Elizabeth stomped off towards the house and Klay followed. Damn-it- all –to-hell! She wasn't going to talk about it! ...Now, a sudden thought struck her: "Whereas, Tabitha never spoke at all. I never talk about my feelings, emotions, or fears. Am I afraid of revealing too much? Feeling too much? Losing control like this? I gloss over any turbulence in my life, preferring not to deal with it on an emotional level. Did Tabitha have a similar fear that any verbal disclosure would make her more vulnerable? Or by giving voice to the situation, it would make it more real, and the truth of it, even more unbearable? Maybe, Tabitha just couldn't face the reality of her own life.

"Please Elizabeth. I don't want to get arrested for creating a public nuisance, but I'm not leaving until we've talked." Elizabeth sank down to the porch step, struggling to maintain her composure.

"It's a personal matter that has to do with my family."

"That's why I want to know about it."

"Why?"

"Because I care about you and I know you're hurting. And you're not talking to anybody about it."

It was a toss; Elizabeth was torn between venting at him or breaking down and crying. Both seemed equally satisfying at this moment.

"If I tell you what's going on, will you promise to leave."

"Afterwards yes, as soon as you want me to."

"When I first got placed in foster care, my sister, Tabitha, and I were placed with my aunt and uncle."

"How many brothers and sisters do you have?"

"All together, I have three sisters and two brothers. But, I have an older brother and sister that I've never even met. Anyway, me and my younger sister, Tabitha, were placed with my aunt and uncle. Later Danielle, my older sister was placed there too."

"What was it like living with your aunt and uncle?"

"It wasn't good! Wade and Evelyn couldn't cope; eventually, they divorced. Danielle ran away, and then, there was just me and Tabitha, staying with Aunt Evelyn. My aunt was abusive and mentally unstable. She definitely didn't like me! Evelyn went to court to terminate her guardianship over me, but she kept Tabitha with her."

"Where is your younger sister now?"

"That's the problem! No one knows where she is or what has happened to her."

"Oh my God, no wonder you're going out of your mind with worry."

"Like I said, Evelyn was unstable. She started roaming from one location to the next with Tabitha. She was staying in a campground, here in Calaveras County in 1992, when some fellow campers saw her physically attack my sister. The police were called and Tabitha was taken into protective custody. The cops took my sister to the hospital to have her examined. My aunt abducted her from the hospital parking lot. Later, Evelyn turns up homeless. She is too crazy to tell anybody what happened to Tabitha after that night."

"Oh, I'm so sorry."

"Then today, this stupid, idiot cop tells me that a picture of my sister was found in the trailer of a serial killer, but they don't know if she's dead or not. No closer to finding her, they just needed me to establish her identity."

"That's horrible! Who was it that told you about the photo?"

"The cop's name is Neal Bryant, and he was completely useless!"

"That's my Dad!" Klay exclaimed in bemusement while Elizabeth looked appalled.

"You've got to be joking!"

"No, I'm not! And my father is not...umm...'a cop.' He's the sheriff of Calaveras county." Klay responded tactfully but clearly rebuffing the insults against his Dad.

"I should say that I'm sorry," came her barbed retort.

"And you should mean it. I understand why you're so hurt and upset. I'd be madder than hell too. However, for the record, Dad is very dogged, but sensible. He wouldn't expose you to this kind of hell, unless he is determined to find the answers. I take it that he may not be forthcoming with all the details, but that doesn't mean he's clueless. Trust me, I know."

"What? Dogged like you."

"Heck no, I'm more of a dog. ...Would you like to take a ride? It might help calm you down."

"I guess, it couldn't hurt. Is it okay if Ellie goes? I could put her out on the patio."

"No, bring her along. She'll enjoy the ride."

"By the way, what brought you to Calaveras, now?"

"The last place Tabitha was seen, was here in 1992. Your 'father' contacted the newsmagazine, 'Mystery Source,' and prompted the producers to create a segment on the serial killer, Eric Morrison, who murdered four little girls in Calaveras during the 1990's. The program emphasized that the 'authorities' believed there was another little girl killed. Your father wanted to identify the unknown child in the photo, which he found in that Creep's trailer.

Then, the 'Sheriff' as good as told me that he wanted a DNA sample from me in case they ever locate a body."

"As I told you Elizabeth, my Dad wouldn't needlessly cause this kind of pain. I'm confident that he is seeking the upshot on your sister's disappearance. I'll talk to him about what's going on. Okay? Now, let's take that ride, so you can relax."

Klay entered the Sheriff's office the next day. The receptionist, Karen, gave him a big smile and got up to open the security door.

"Klay, it's been such a long time since I've seen you. Are you still attending the university?" Karen asked, giving him an affectionate hug and led him into the office.

"Yes, I still have a year to go for my bachelor's; then, there's grad school. I'm not quite to the finish line, yet. Just enjoying my summer break. Is Dad around?"

"Yes, I'll tell him you are here." Karen picked up the phone, "Neal, your son, Klay is here to see you. ..."Klay, you can go on back."

"Thank you Karen, it's wonderful seeing you."

Neal stood up as Klay entered his office. "Hi Klay, what's up?"

"Dad, I need to talk to you." He said as he sat down across the desk from his father.

"Okay, what's going on?" Neal inquired as he noted Klay's solemn expression.

"You know, I went to dinner with Jeannie and her family on Sunday. At dinner, we meet a young lady, Elizabeth. We invited her to have dinner with us. I've been seeing her; we're dating."

"Okay," Neal was still perplexed.

"Last night when I went to see Elizabeth, she was extremely broken up; out-of-her-mind with grief."

"Yes."

"She indicated that 'you' spotlighted this story about a missing victim of Eric Morrison on a national television program because you wanted to establish the identity of an unknown child in a photo that belonged to Morrison. You dredged up this tragedy in order to get a DNA sample from a family member. Just in case you eventually locate a body. I told her that you simply weren't like that. You wouldn't open this kind of wound unless you were prepared to find answers. Please tell me, I spoke the truth."

"Oh, I see," Neal said finally making the connection, looking dismayed. He paused to collect his thoughts before answering.

"Klay, it's complicated!" Neal said, rubbing the bridge of his nose. Back in 1998 when we were investigating this serial murder case, we had reason to believe there was another victim. But, we couldn't find any trace of this child. Therefore, we had a 'lost' child that would never be found or identified. Some family would never know the fate of their poor, little girl. This outcome never sat well with me! And it's something that has been very hard for me to let go of."

"Yes Dad, I can see how it would bother you."

"Last year, we located Morrison's trailer. There were numerous photos of his known victims, both before and after their deaths. However, there was only one picture of a girl that we couldn't identify. This child was alive at the time of the photo. There were no photos of her death as there were with the other girls. ....You know damn well, I was going to follow up, and try to find out what happened to her. Excuse my language! But you can bet your ass that if there is any way to find the answers to the child's whereabouts, I'm going to pursue it."

"Thanks, Dad, I needed to hear it for Elizabeth's sake. She is

41

hurting."

"I hated putting her through the wringer, I feel for your friend, Elizabeth. Any family in this type of situation goes through a living hell. But I've got to warn you Klay, we never found any trace of Tabitha back during the investigation. And now ten years have passed, it is likely that we've lost any trail of evidence in order to find her. I wish I had a better answer than that for you."

"I wish the prognosis was better too."

"I believe that Elizabeth has had more than her fair share of problems already, and I certainly don't want to add to them," Neil commented.

"You can say that again. I've just heard bits and pieces about her childhood and it sucked. Thanks, Dad for leveling with me. I'll see you later at home."

"See you, then."

Neil watched his son leave. The coincidence of his son striking up a relationship with a girl, which was involved in one of his cases, especially this one was unreal. It was an uncomfortable feeling when his professional and personal life collided like this had. He had always tried to keep his professional life completely separate. Again, he would have to be careful to maintain healthy boundaries in this matter.

After leaving his Dad's office, Klay picked up two coffees and then, drove directly over to Marion's house to talk to Elizabeth. She opened the door, more quickly this time.

"Hi Elizabeth, how are you doing today?" He handed her a coffee cup.

"My mood has improved somewhat since yesterday. Thanks for the coffee."

"I just spoke to my Dad. Could we sit out back and I'll tell you about our conversation?" Klay asked carefully as he noted Elizabeth's guarded stance.

"Alright." Elizabeth led the way to the backyard with Ellie at her side.

They both seated themselves in a lawn chair and Klay started to speak.

"From what Dad told me, during their original investigation of the serial murders, he strongly suspected that there was another victim out there. But despite the effort, no evidence or trace of this child was found. He was obsessed with the thought that this child may be lost forever. Then three years later, they find Eric Morrison's trailer with a picture of an unknown child. He is determined to find out what happened to Tabitha, but he also knows it may be an impossible task."

"I guess I feel better about his 'position' then I did yesterday. He really seems to care about what happened to Tabitha."

"He also felt bad about putting you through that interview, but he felt it was his only option for gaining any ground on Tabitha's status or whereabouts."

"Okay, I can accept that explanation. But, I've been hung-up on a question since I first saw the segment aired on *'Mystery Source.'* Your father has been convinced that another child was 'lost' out there since he investigated in 1998; he told the news program that, he told you and me the same thing. But, there was never any evidence or trace of another girl until this photo surfaced in 2001. What made him so certain?"

"I don't know. He never said why he believed there was another victim. You're right that is weird."

"I have a feeling that 'whatever' convinced your dad initially that there was another victim out, may be the key to finding Tabitha. I have to find out what the basis was, for his reasoning, because I need to find my sister!"

"I believe we need to go back and talk to Dad again to get to the bottom of this situation."

"Thanks, Klay, I know this isn't your battle."

"It is now," he said with a slight smile.

CHAPTER 3

Adjacent to Klay, Elizabeth sat across the desk from Sheriff Neal Bryant in the claustrophobic office.

"Sorry, I took off like that yesterday. I was upset." Elizabeth managed a stiff apology.

"I understand. What can I do to help you?" Despite Bryant's civil response, Elizabeth thought his expression appeared guarded. Was she just being paranoid? Elizabeth questioned her own hyper-vigilant observation.

"During the investigation into those murders, you were convinced that there was 'a fifth victim;' not that there could be additional victims. You 'specified' that there was one more possible victim. At the time, you hadn't found the photo of my sister or any other evidence. What is going on? Why were you so sure?" Elizabeth abruptly inquired, she noted that Bryant looked uneasy as he subtly shifted his position in his chair. Elizabeth knew her assumption was right on target. Bryant was being less than forthcoming as he seemed to search for a plausible explanation. He was going to feed her a line of bullshit.

"Listen, this is my sister, we're talking about; I've got the right to know! Whatever convinced you that there was a fifth victim might be key to solving her disappearance." Elizabeth rankled, her voice growing louder under her steadfast glare.

"Serial killers follow certain patterns and routines in their killings which become their signature and that helps us to identify them. Based on Morrison's time frame between killing cycles and other small indicators, these factors seemed to imply that there was perhaps another victim." Bryant offered what Elizabeth knew amounted to 'professional dribble;' or double speak. He appeared to answer the question without saying a God-damn thing.

"I'm not buying it! No evidence, circumstantial or otherwise, but this investigation continued to haunt you after the fact." She was irked with his flimsy accounting. ..."I can see it in your face; you're holding something back. Why can't you tell me? It's my sister for god sake."

"I don't know what to tell you. If we had something solid back in 1998 to follow up on; we would have continued to investigate. We did question Morrison, but it lead nowhere. He would never admit to nor deny the existence of a fifth victim."

"I don't believe you. There is something you're hiding; that's my gut reaction. I'm going to find a way to pursue this matter. Thanks for seeing me." Elizabeth stated insincerely, as she abruptly left his office for the second time.

"Now what?" Klay inquired after catching up to Elizabeth. He had made brief amends to his father before leaving the office, himself.

"Only God knows!" Elizabeth exclaimed in frustration. "There has to be a way to review the investigation. Your father isn't going to let me see the file. Can't you see he wasn't giving me the whole truth; he was just trying to pacify me. Cops and social workers are always skirting around issues when they are trying to avoid giving you the straight scoop."

"Okay, but what can you do at this point?" Klay responded neutrally.

"I'll call that Center for Missing Children. Maybe they can give me something to do, going forward. I just hope they're not too entrenched with the cops," she replied bitterly.

Klay waited on the back patio as Elizabeth went inside the house to make her call.

A while later, Elizabeth returned to the patio.

"What did the center tell you?"

I was able to talk to this guy, Trenton, from the regional office in Palo Alto. He told me that sometimes a family member hires a lawyer, and the lawyer can petition the court to review the investigative records. Occasionally, a family member will petition the court to ask for access to these files; but it usually isn't done that way. Their agency doesn't provide legal services but can help with other services. He said he would send a list of resources and available services. He also gave me a number to a foundation for missing children. I spoke to a woman there. She told me that they had an attorney who occasionally works pro bono to assist in certain situations. She will ask if this attorney if she's willing to help me. Either she or this attorney will call me back in the next few days."

"It sounds as if you're making progress. I better get going; I've got some errands to do. I'll take you out later to grab a bite to eat if you're up to it."

"Thanks that would be fine," Elizabeth said absent-mindedly.

A week later, Elizabeth arrived for her scheduled appointment with the attorney, Cheryl Weiss, in Acacia. Cheryl was a heavyset, blond woman in her late forties with a no nonsense attitude. Again for the lawyer, Elizabeth recapped the case history involving her Aunt Evelyn and the disappearance of her sister Tabitha. Then, Elizabeth told Cheryl about the photo of Tabitha that the serial killer -Morrison had in his trailer. She outlined the information given by Bryant during their two conversations.

"Bryant knew there had been another victim before he found that photo of my sister," Elizabeth reiterated her main contention. "He will not give me a significant reason for this assumption. He said he doesn't know if my sister Tabitha is alive or dead; or if he will ever find her. I don't see any reason that he cannot give me the complete accounting at this point,"

"If the Sheriff finds out that Eric Morrison killed or harmed your sister in any way, he could file additional charges. It could mean the death penalty. He may not want to compromise any future prosecution." Cheryl suggested.

"Bryant has already indicated that he couldn't find any trace of evidence in relation to my sister and that it was highly unlikely that he would at this late date. According to Bryant, the only connection between that Creep and my sister was the photo. Bryant couldn't say when or how my sister met up with Morrison. I honestly doubt my having access to these records will hinder anything."

"Or in any way help you to locate your sister?" Cheryl finished her unspoken thought, giving voice to her private fear.

"I think Bryant was hiding something in the investigation. It may be nothing that will help me find Tabitha. Obviously, Bryant wasn't able to get a lead from whatever information, he has. But unless I know everything, I won't be satisfied that I've tried everything to find her. I owe it to Tabitha!"

"I can't promise you that I'll be successful, but I will file a petition. If the court grants the request, I'll review the investigation and report any irregularities to you.

"Thanks for your help," Elizabeth said as she got up to leave.

Elizabeth arrived at Marion's house. Should she give Klay a call and tell him about her meeting with Cheryl Weiss? No, it wasn't necessary; she'd catch up with him later. But almost as soon as she walked through the door, the phone rang.

"Hello?"

"Hi Elizabeth, just calling to see how your meeting went?" It was Klay.

"Alright. The attorney, Cheryl Weiss, is going to see if the court will give her permission to review the investigation. But, she wasn't optimistic that we'd find anything useful."

"Well, at least, it's something."

"Yes, I guess so. Hey Klay, can I call you back later? I need to go check on Ellie."

"Sure, talk to you later."

As Elizabeth was letting Ellie through the patio door. The phone rang again. Not Klay, again! She answered the phone with an exacerbated, "hello."

"Hello, could I speak to Elizabeth Lenard?"

"This is Elizabeth."

"Officer Crawford, here. I'm calling to let you know that we've received the age progressed photo of your sister from the NCMEC. I'd like to schedule an appointment with you to review the photo and the flyer information before it's sent out nationally. I can meet with you after three today, or first thing tomorrow morning."

"I can be at your office at three."

"Okay, I'll see you then."

At least this time, Elizabeth didn't have to wait. She was quickly lead back to an office by the cop-Crawford.

Elizabeth apprehensively sat down across from Crawford, subconsciously gripping the armrests of the office chair. She remained silent, waiting for him to speak.

Crawford cleared his throat. "Here is the age advanced image of your sister. We'll place this picture, adjacent to a photo of Tabitha at age seven. I've included the logistical information about your sister that we plan to circulate. We didn't include any information about your aunt, since we know that your sister isn't with her at this time. Our hope is that by excluding this information, it may open up new leads involving Tabitha's disappearance." He picked up a manila file folder and handed it over to Elizabeth.

Elizabeth slowly reached up to take the folder. Nervously, she held the folder, half anticipating and half dreading to look inside at the contents. All she wanted to see right now was the photo, and yet she didn't. Staring at the folder, Elizabeth pictured Tabitha. In her mind, Tabitha was still that delicate little girl with a quiet, vacant demeanor. Elizabeth remembered her soft, dusky blond hair and solemn blue, downcast eyes. Gearing herself up, Elizabeth tentatively opened the folder and stared, mesmerized by the picture in front of her.

The replica of her sweet, little sister had morphed into a girl of late adolescence. The teen had light brown hair, and her deep-set, blue eyes didn't appear as prominent in her facial features now. Stunned, Elizabeth realized this image bore a striking resemblance to herself. She had never recalled any similarity between her appearance and that of Tabitha's, maybe because their coloring was so different. Also, Elizabeth had failed to realize how close in age, they actually were. Somehow, Tabitha had always seemed so much younger. Her sister had been so incredibly vulnerable that Elizabeth though of her as a baby and tended to mother her to death. She'd been so bossy with Tabitha. What would their relationship be like today, if Tabitha was still around?

Contemplating the image, tears misted Elizabeth's eyes but quickly receded, and vanished behind her closed lids. "Oh God, Tabitha. It's all my fault! But, I promise I'm going to make it right. I'll find you; you know I will," Elizabeth silently vowed. Then, she absently reviewed the information on the flyer. It was all demographic; birthdate, the date of Tabitha's disappearance, general description, and contact information.

"The image and the information seem fine," Elizabeth said tersely, looking blankly at Officer Crawford.

"Did your sister have any scars or birthmarks?" Crawford inquired.

"No. ...Wait, she had an oblong birthmark on her left shoulder. I use to draw a flower around it with a leafy stem. We'd pretend it was a tattoo or something." Elizabeth continued on as if speaking to herself, giving voice to this elusive memory.

"Good, we'll add that data. Can you think of any other unique markings?" When Elizabeth shook her head in the negative, Crawford responded, "Then we'll update this flyer and get it disseminated."

"Could I please get a copy of this picture?" Elizabeth asked with a slight tremor in her voice as she handed the age progressed photo back to Crawford.

"Yes, of course," came his prompt reply.

Two weeks later, Elizabeth received a call back from Cheryl Weiss. The attorney had reviewed the criminal investigation into the four murders committed by Eric Morrison. She then had summarized the case, along with the supporting evidence in a legal brief. There was also an addendum, which included a brief synopsis of statements given by individuals who were parties or possible witnesses to the proceedings. However, the defendant, Eric Morrison, had made a plea bargain agreement in the case to avoid the death penalty. So the case never went to trial. Great, thought Elizabeth, she uses legalese and expects everyone to understand it, but Elizabeth got the essence of what she was saying. Cheryl arranged to meet with her for an hour tomorrow to discuss the investigation and to give her a hard copy of her summary on the case. Or as Cheryl called it, 'her legal brief.'

Now, Elizabeth was sitting across from Cheryl in her Acacia office. Her immense gratitude to the lawyer, gradually transforming into frustration and anger at what Elizabeth perceived as the lawyer's 'stonewalling' tactics.

"I want to read through the investigation myself," Elizabeth demanded indignantly.

"No, I told you that I had reviewed the file. I'm more than competent to analyze investigative material and detect any problems or discrepancies. That is how you prepare for criminal trials."

"Why can't I see the file? The investigation is over."

"Listen Elizabeth, I'm not going to argue this point with you," Cheryl stated curtly, hiding her empathetic reaction towards the young woman in front of her. Her brusque bravado seemed to mask a very sensitive and vulnerable nature. "You have my brief; it's not necessary for you to examine the file yourself."

Elizabeth continued to stare Cheryl down, stubbornly defying the lawyer's resolute declaration. Cheryl intuitively switched gears, trying to mitigate the escalating confrontation. "Elizabeth, ...there are many graphic photos, evidentiary materials, and other descriptive details involving the victims; you should 'NEVER' see. The kind of 'nasty' that no one, especially a family member, should ever have to view or even think about. And, it will not help you to locate your sister. In the investigation, the only indicator as to the existence of a fifth victim seemed to be the amount of time between the first and second known murders. As Bryant reported, the time lapse didn't seem to fit into Morrison's pattern."

"Bryant was definitely worried about something in the file. He became uptight, when I questioned him about what he was hiding. Was there anything strange or weird about this investigation?"

The only oddity, I detected, was that Sheriff Bryant had hired this woman, Alyssa Sullivan, who had discovered the body of Amy George. Ms. Sullivan was also, present when the body of Bree Jamison was located. She was definitely a viable witness before Bryant hired her. It was highly unusual that any investigator would hire an individual who possibly could be called as a witness in the trial."

"Why do you think Bryant hired this woman? She must be mixed up or enmeshed in the investigation somehow."

"I didn't say that. I don't know why Sheriff Bryant hired this woman. The Sheriff's office completed a complete criminal background check on this woman and her husband. Everything appeared to be in order. "

"Why was the husband checked out?" Elizabeth suspiciously inquired.

"He (David Sullivan) was present and with Alyssa Sullivan when the body of the first victim was discovered. This is all I can do for you. You are welcome to give me a call if anything else materializes in your sister's case."

"Thanks for your help," Elizabeth said uncomfortably as she took a large envelope from Cheryl.

After leaving the attorney's office, Elizabeth found a nearby, city library. She sat down in a secluded area and studied Cheryl's brief. Subsequently, Elizabeth researched all the media reports and newspaper accounts involving Eric Morrison and the related murders. She made copies of any relevant or noteworthy articles, before making her way out the door.

Elizabeth immediately drove straight to the Sheriff's office. She waited over twenty minutes, becoming increasingly more agitated while she waited to see Bryant. He seemed disinclined to show her back into the interior office; but relented, when Elizabeth insisted that she needed to speak with him.

"How can I help you, Ms. Lenard?" Neal Bryant asked after they were seated.

"Who the hell is Alyssa Sullivan? Why was she involved in the investigation into those murders?" Elizabeth saw Bryant recoil slightly under the weight of her questions. She knew she'd struck a nerve. It seemed apparent there was something unseemly about that woman's connection to this case.

"Ms. Sullivan was an intern for our office, who provided some additional research and general assistance throughout the Morrison investigation."

"This woman discovered the first body and was a possible witness. Why was she then hired by the Sheriff's Department?"

"Excuse me, my staffing decisions are none of your business;" Neal replied bluntly.

"This Sullivan woman finds two bodies within a couple of months; after Morrison slid underneath the radar and got away with all those murders for almost ten years. She must be associated with that Creep in some way!"

"You don't know what the hell you're talking about," Neal clipped.

"And you're covering up for her!"

"For your information even though it's none of your damn business, Alyssa Sullivan and her family relocated to California, years after the murders took place. She had no connection to Morrison or any of the victims, whatsoever. Your lawyer must have told you that a comprehensive criminal background check was conducted on Ms. Sullivan, and the Department of Justice cleared her.   Hell, Alyssa was even injured and put her life on the line in order to apprehend Morrison."

"It makes absolutely no sense that you chose to hire this woman for the internship; right after she discovers the first body. You're covering up something," Elizabeth rejoined.

"And I told you, our staffing issues are not open for discussion. Alyssa Sullivan's employment with our department has nothing to do with your sister's disappearance or whereabouts. Now, I will show you out because I have other business matters to attend to."

As Elizabeth pulled up to Marion's place, she saw that Klay's car was parked in front of Jeannie's house. He must have been watching for her because he called out to her as she approached the front door.

"Hey Elizabeth," he hurried across the street to join her. "You met with a lawyer today, right? How did it go?"

She was still amped up from her heated exchange with Bryant. How could she calmly discuss this criminal investigation with Klay? Hell, Bryant was his father. Elizabeth sank down to sit on the porch step.

"I don't think your father likes me very much right now and I'm afraid the feeling is mutual."

"Wait, you mean you talked to my dad today."

"Yes, but it was more like I argued with him."

"Okay, tell me what you fought about."

"First, I should tell you about my meeting with Cheryl Weiss. She reviewed and summarized the criminal case against Eric Morrison for me. I told her that I wanted to review the investigation myself. She refused, saying that the investigation was too gruesome and wouldn't help me find Tabitha in any way. She reiterated what your dad said about time gap between the first and second murder was way too long. This gap didn't seem to fit Morrison's killing pattern. There didn't seem to be any other information or evidence to indicate any more killings by Morrison."

"That follows what Dad told us."

"However, Cheryl indicated that it was peculiar that the individual that discovered the first body, was also, present when the second body was located. Then, this woman was quickly hired by your father to work for the Sheriff's office. Something was very unusual about her involvement in this case."

"I admit, it does seem a little strange."

"Later, I challenged your father about this woman's association with this case. I told him she must be connected with the murders, and he was covering up her involvement."

"Now, I don't know why he'd get uptight about those assertions," Klay replied ironically. "C'mon Elizabeth, get real."

"Okay, I admit what I said was a bit much. But, I could tell from his response that there was something he's hiding regarding Alyssa Sullivan's connection to this investigation." Elizabeth retorted hotly.

"I agree with you that there must be some 'unique reason' that Dad brought this woman into the case. And whatever his reason was, he doesn't want it publicly known. But, that doesn't mean anything unscrupulous was going on."

"Of course, you're going to say that Klay; he's your dad!"

"Look at the big picture, Morrison kills four children over a ten year time frame and doesn't get caught. This woman, Sullivan, discovers the first body and Dad brings her into the investigation. Within a few months, these other murders are uncovered, and the killer is apprehended. I'd contend that Dad must have done something right to get those results. And this woman cannot be in league with Morrison if he is now behind bars."

"I see your point," she replied, reluctant to drop the matter.

"Elizabeth, whatever the situation with Alyssa Sullivan is; it doesn't seem to be connected with your sister's disappearance. You don't want to get so caught up in squabbling over details that you lose sight of your goal, which is to find your sister. Please don't take this the wrong way, because I'm trying to help you. But, you probably shouldn't place yourself at odds with anyone who can help you in terms of Tabitha's case. "

Elizabeth was ruffled, but she knew Klay was right. It was simple common sense. She had let her temper get the best of her.

"Advice taken; you've given me a good reality check."

"Okay, then let's go and grab a quick bite to eat. I'm starving," Klay said, holding out his arm to help her up from the porch.

Elizabeth was at a standstill. What action could she possibly take to make progress in Tabitha's case? She couldn't play the waiting game. She'd waited long enough already. In frustration, she once again skimmed the legal brief, looking for who knows what? She perused the information about the young victims of Eric Morrison. The childhood backgrounds of these girls sounded all too common to someone like her, who aged out of the foster care system. Elizabeth easily could see how Tabitha, same as these other kids, would have been easy pickings for a Creep like Morrison. Her Mom had been incarcerated in prison at the time with no father in the picture. And then, Aunt Evelyn could not even take care of and protect herself, let alone a six-year-old kid. Where were the mothers of these young children?

Scrutinizing the brief, Elizabeth found out that the mothers of both Shilo Wilson and Amy George were now deceased, and Priscilla's mother was incarcerated in prison. But, the mother of Bree Jamison still lived within the county. Then, it occurred to Elizabeth that she could contact Crystal Jamison and get her perspective on the investigation. It would likely be a useless gesture. But regardless of her conversation with Klay, she still had reservations about what role Alyssa Sullivan played in the investigation. Could this hidden detail impact the outcome of her sister's case? She would never know unless she had the answers.

Elizabeth looked up the name, Crystal Jamison, in the phone directory and found an address. She had to see Crystal in person to make this kind of inquiry. She just hoped that the woman hadn't moved. She couldn't find the street on the map in the phone directory; she'd have to pick up a county map. Elizabeth got ready to leave by taking Ellie out to the patio.

Was this Crystal Jamison's house? The residence was set well back from a rural, unpaved road, giving Elizabeth an unsettled feeling. She suspiciously eyed the isolated house, looking vigilantly for any signs of snarling guard dogs or other possible hazards. The aged home looked neglected as if it could use a good coat of paint. But as she drew closer, the house looked comfortably cheerful with potted flowers adorning the porch and kid's toys, and bikes were scattered about the yard. Elizabeth visibly relaxed her guard as she approached the front door and knocked. Someone looked out from behind the closed, window blinds. Then, a woman in her thirties with dark, straight hair opened the door a crack, peering out at Elizabeth with a distrustful expression. She clearly didn't like unexpected visitors at her door, but she seemed to relax her guard as she took in Elizabeth's youthful appearance.

"Hello, how can I help you?"

"Hi, my name is Elizabeth Lenard. I was hoping to talk to Crystal Jamison. Is this her residence?"

The woman eyed her curiously and responded, "I'm Crystal (Jamison) Moyers."

"I'm sorry to bother you but I hope you'll be willing to talk to me."

"What do you want to talk to me for?" Crystal questioned, wary of her intentions.

"Umm...this is difficult matter to talk about. My younger sister, Tabitha, went missing in 1992 from Calaveras County. She disappeared almost ten years ago, and she hasn't been seen since that time. I'm trying to find her." Elizabeth fought to keep her voice steady and maintain her composure. She saw the compassion and understanding dawn in Crystal's expression.

"I'm sorry about your sister. But, how can I help you?"

"Can we sit down out here on the porch and talk? I know it can't be easy for you, either."

"Alright," she opened the door wider and stepped out onto the porch, supporting an infant on her hip." Crystal gestured to one of the lawn chairs and said, "Have a seat."

Elizabeth sat down in a chair and stared blankly straight ahead, not looking at Crystal as she took the chair next to her.

"Tabitha was living with my Aunt Evelyn, who had legal guardianship. They were staying in a campground in Calaveras. The police took Tabitha into protective custody; because my crazy Aunt had left my sister alone for several hours without warm clothes or even a blanket. The neighboring campers were worried about Tabitha. These campers told Tabitha to come into their tent, so she could keep warm. When Evelyn returned, she was mad at Tabitha for disobeying her by 'mixing with those people.' My aunt started beating the crap out of Tabitha and the police were called."

"Why didn't your Aunt like the other campers?" Crystal asked curiously.

"I don't know that was just in the police report. But, Evelyn didn't need an excuse. She was paranoid and crazy to boot!" Crystal nodded, and Elizabeth continued.

"My aunt found out that the social worker took Tabitha to the hospital. Later that night, Evelyn grabbed Tabitha from the hospital visitor lot and took off with her. A few years ago, my Aunt Evelyn was found homeless, living on the streets. She was placed in a mental health facility and was unable to tell anyone what happened to my sister. Last year, the sheriff -Bryant found a photo of Tabitha in an abandoned trailer, which belonged to Eric Morrison."

"Oh my God," Crystal cried out, the tears and pain evident as she tried to stifle her sobs. Elizabeth struggled to rein in her emotions as she continued.

"I don't know if Tabitha is still alive or not. Bryant couldn't find any evidence of her death or any leads to follow. Nothing but that photo. I don't know what to do now. I read a summary of the criminal investigation of Eric Morrison; nothing stood out in regards to my sister. But, Alyssa Sullivan seemed to be extremely involved in the investigation; I wondered if you had ever met her?"

"Oh yes," Crystal smiled through her tears. "I named my baby here, after her, Alyssa."

"This woman -Alyssa Sullivan found the body of the first child at that mining camp." Elizabeth lowered her voice and continued softly, then Ms. Sullivan was with Bryant when your daughter was found. A couple of weeks later, Bryant hired her to work on this investigation. Did she ever tell you why she was hired by the Sheriff's office?"

"Wow, I didn't know she went to work for the Sheriff's Office."

"She was hired only for a few months in a temporary internship during the Morrison investigation. How did you meet Alyssa Sullivan?"

"I met Ally in the lobby of the Sheriff's station. She was waiting to talk to Sheriff Bryant and give him information about the murders. I guess you don't know it, but she's a psychic. She was having dreams about my little girl, Bree, and talking with her."

"You don't believe that, do you?" What the hell! Elizabeth was flabbergasted; this was unreal. It had to be a joke.

"Yes, I believe her. She knew all kinds of things about Bree that she wouldn't have found out about otherwise. At first, I was very jealous because I wanted my baby to come back to me. But, I came to accept it. Some people just have that natural gift. I've often thought that maybe Bree found it impossible to reach me because I was too torn up over her loss. I was out-of-my -mind with grief."

"I'm sorry, you lost your child. I wish it could have worked out differently."

"So do I. I hope you find Tabitha safe and sound. I'll say a prayer for your family."

"Thanks for talking to me."

"You really should talk to Ally; she might be able to get a read on your sister."

"I'll think about it. I'm not sure I'm into this psychic stuff." Really, Elizabeth thought to herself.

"If you talk to Ally, she'll change your mind."

Again, Elizabeth drove straight to the Sheriff's station, after leaving Crystal's house. Bryant was in the parking lot, getting into the sheriff's cruiser when Elizabeth pulled in. She marched up to Bryant with her hand on her hips.

"I need to talk to you!" Elizabeth demanded unceremoniously.

"And I need to leave for an appointment, besides there is no new information that I can offer you at this time."

"What's the truth behind this cock and bull story that you hired a 'psychic' to work on the Morrison case?" Neal Bryant was stunned. He shifted his gaze, trying to disguise his discomfort.

"What in the world are you talking about?"

"Alyssa Sullivan. Is it true that she was feeding you information about these murders?"

"As you are aware, Alyssa Sullivan worked on this case and very diligently and persistently worked towards the apprehension of Eric Morrison. In the process, she could have been killed, and her family's safety was compromised. Our office owes her a debt of gratitude for her service."

"Did you hire her for her wealth of psychic abilities? What a crock!"

"Honestly, I don't care what you believe or disbelieve. I am extremely sorry that I can't tell you what happened to your sister at this time. At this point, you know as much as I do about the criminal investigation. Our conversation is done; I have a scheduled meeting to get to."

"I want to meet with this woman, Alyssa Sullivan."

"I don't think it's advisable."

"What are you afraid of?"

"Ally isn't employed with our department anymore. I can ask if she's willing to meet with you, but I am going to advise her against it." Bryant said as he closed the car door.

CHAPTER 4

When Neal returned to his office in the early afternoon, he telephoned Alyssa Sullivan.

"Hello Ally, this is Neal," he said when she answered the phone.

"Hi Neal. How are you doing?"

"Listen Ally, I've got a problem," came Neal's curt reply.

"What is it?" Ally asked in concern. Neal's typical calm and easy-going manner was now, unusually ruffled.

"It's one -Elizabeth Lenard; she truly is a real pain in the neck."

"Okay. Who is Elizabeth Lenard? And how did she manage to ruffle your feathers?" Ally chortled; this was so unlike Neal.

"Remember, I told you about the photo that we found in Eric Morrison's trailer?"

"Yes," said Ally, instantly subdued.

"Well, I was able to get that news program to do a segment on Morrison and report the possibility of an unknown fifth victim. I didn't want to simply air the photo on the show because we don't know the status of this child. Elizabeth Lenard came in with a picture of her little sister, who went missing in 1992 from this county. It's a ringer for the child in Morrison's photo."

"Why didn't this child's information come up in our investigation, when we searched for missing girls from this area?"

"I can only speculate. The child, Tabitha Lenard, was staying with her aunt at a local campground; they were not from Calaveras County. The child was removed from her aunt's custody due to physical abuse. Later on the same night as this incident of abuse, the aunt absconded with the child. It took several days to figure out the true identity of the aunt, Evelyn Heald, who had guardianship of the little girl, because Ms. Heald gave a bogus identification card to the police. A national search was initiated, but I believe the missing child case was transferred back to Sheldon, California, which was were Ms. Heald, last resided.

"Okay. But, how did Eric Morrison get a hold of Tabitha?"

"I don't have a clue. I believe Ms. Heald and Tabitha arrived in Calaveras County on the same day as the abduction. Many years later, Ms. Heald was found living on the streets, homeless, when she was arrested. She's been deemed mentally incompetent to stand trial by the courts. She is institutionalized in a mental health facility until she is lucid enough to participate in her own defense. Whether it's an act or not; Ms. Heald cannot account for Tabitha's whereabouts."

"How horrible is that!" Why is the sister making these inquiries? Where are the parents?"

"I don't know. This girl was in the foster care system; she must have been in the system for a reason. In fact, I believe she has several siblings, all of which were all placed in foster care."

"How old is she?"

"About nineteen, I guess."

"Oh ... the poor girl."

"The girl is no shrinking violet. She's been yanking my chain."

"What's she doing exactly?"

"Rude, defiant, angry! From the get-go, she been all up in my face demanding answers. I told her everything I know, but she even got a lawyer involved.   She's accused me of everything from being indifferent to being party to a cover up for God's sake. ...Worst yet, she's been dating my son, Klay. Serendipity, I don't have a clue about how that happened! But, she has him all up-in-arms to boot."

"I'm sorry; it sounds like a mess. I know you didn't call me just to vent. How can I help?"

"She is suspicious of you and your involvement in the investigation. Then, I don't know how, but she found out about your psychic abilities. She doesn't believe in the paranormal but rather still, thinks you are somehow complicit in the crimes. She wants to meet with you. I told her I was against it, but I think she'll try to contact you."

"Then it's better if we head her off at the pass, and I'll meet with her in your office."

"Ally. ... "

"Neal you said it yourself, she's not going to be content until she meets me.

"I don't know what this girl's going to do next or what to expect from her!"

"I don't know what she expects from me either, but I'd rather face it straight on. Besides Neal, I think you're being too hard on the girl. I think I understand Elizabeth...She's hurt deep and cannot let her guard down. Her anger is the only defense that she's got, against the grief. Elizabeth has always had to handle everything on her own and cannot accept or trust any reliance on others. She resents anyone in authority for they have failed her in the past. Yes Neal, she has a chip on her shoulder and is probably trying to see past it. Elizabeth sounds a lot like Terri, a young woman that I worked with through Family Preservation Services. Given time and patience, I believe Elizabeth may come around.

"Alright. But remember, I did try to warn you. I'll call and schedule an appointment. What is your schedule like on Thursday?"

"I'm open before lunch."

"Okay, I'll call you back later with the time."

Ally was seated in Neal's office on Thursday, when Neal brought Elizabeth into the room. Ally stood up and offered her hand.

"Hi, I'm Ally and you must be Elizabeth." Elizabeth, ignored the handshake, crossing her arms defiantly as she continued to stare balefully at Ally.

Ally sat down and leaned towards Elizabeth. "Neal told me about the situation. I'm so sorry about Tabitha. I'm praying that some additional information comes forward."

"You're a psychic, you tell me where she's at," Elizabeth said contemptuously. Then, she continued snidely, "Where's your crystal ball?"

"Actually, I've never seen a real crystal ball. I wonder if they work," Ally replied with a slight smile, not affronted by Elizabeth's sarcasm. When Elizabeth failed to respond, Ally continued considering how to proceed.

"I understand that you've been uneasy about my involvement in this case. I might be suspicious if I were you too. Let me explain to you what happened from the beginning. You may want to sit down; this may take a while." Elizabeth ignored the suggestion.

"I'll start off my telling you that I moved to California with my husband in September 1995. I didn't know the killer, any of the victims; or anyone associated with the investigation at that time. Nor do I have any relatives, who lived with in the area prior to 1996. I'm sure you know that a criminal background check was completed on both me and my husband prior to my internship with the department. Also, I'm not a 'typical' psychic; one who has a series of psychic intervals. I had '*a*' psychic episode. I don't know how or why it happened to me."

"How convenient; what a likely story!" Elizabeth was flabbergasted, was she really supposed to shallow this line of bullshit.

"Elizabeth, I can only tell you what happened. In fact, initially, I and especially my husband had a difficult time accepting my psychic visions and perceptions. You can choose to believe or not to; I'm not going to try and convince you one way or the other. "

"That's good because I'm not buying into this crap," Elizabeth said petulantly. She slid down into the chair but held her defensive posture.

"It was March 1998, when my husband and I went for a car ride. We were traveling through the rural area called, 'Horseshoe Bend' on our way to the reservoir. My husband, David, stopped to read a map, when I saw a child running in the meadow. I started to worry if the girl was lost but then, I couldn't see her anymore. I didn't know where she'd gone.

"Really?" Elizabeth asked facetiously.

"After that sighting, I started having some terrible nightmares about this child. I found out that the dead body of Shilo Wilson was found in the meadow at Horseshoe Bend in 1989. I wondered if I saw a ghost, because I couldn't understand why I kept having nightmares about this particular girl. I went to the library and found a photo of Shilo in the newspaper, but it was not the same child I saw. Later, I found a missing child flyer of Bree Jamison. This photo was of the girl that I observed in the meadow, and I was still having nightmares about her."

Ally cleared her throat, "I didn't know what to do. I'd never had any psychic experiences before this time, and I didn't think anyone would believe me. At the time, I was nine months pregnant; ready to go into labor at any minute. So my husband, despite his uncertainty, agreed to take me back to 'Horseshoe Bend.' David was way more skeptical then you; he thought I was absolutely nuts!" Responding to Ally's statement, Elizabeth raised her eyebrows and gave a slight nod.

"Uh huh."

"Anyway...we found skeletal remains up at the Animas mine site, above the meadow. We contacted the Sheriff's Office, and Neal responded to this call. Several weeks later, I was watching the news. The broadcaster reported that the skeletal remains (that my husband

and I found) belonged to Amy George, and showed a picture of this child. The girl didn't resemble Bree Jamison; then I knew Bree's body still must be undiscovered within that area."

Ally looked at Elizabeth; who hadn't changed her uncompromising posture. The girl stared at her with a blank expression.

"Finally, I contacted Neal and leveled with him. I told him about all the dreams and visions that I'd had. Initially, Neal also believed that I could be involved in the crime in some way. However, I started receiving even stronger visions and messages from Bree Jamison. Bree showed me where her body would be found, and started filtering information about the killer to me. Bree also indicated that there were four more children with her, but this information was rather vague on the details."

Ally nodded at Neal, "Based on my clean background check, and the accuracy of the information I was able to provide, Neal came to accept the veracity of my psychic visions. But, Neal didn't want to publicly acknowledge that I had these 'supernatural' insights because he knew it would hinder the prosecution of the killer. Similar to yourself, many people in the general public have a difficult time accepting the truth of any psychic or intuitive experience. Neal also wanted to utilize any factors or other information that I could contribute, to help to identify and apprehend the killer. Therefore, he hired me as an intern. It worked! Within a couple of months, Eric Morrison was identified, apprehended, and subsequently plea bargained to the murders."

"Whatever," Elizabeth replied sardonically.

"Do you have any questions that you want to ask me?"

"If all these 'psychic' things were going on, why didn't you know if you'd found all the bodies or not?"

"This psychic or intuitive process in difficult to describe or explain. Many of the visions were very short and disjointed; sometimes very hard to understand. Moreover, I had no control over whether or not I received the visions or what information came across to me. I did try to direct or structure some of the information I received from Bree, with varying degrees of success. "

"Fine."

"And this is going to sound even crazier to you. When I first met Bree, she was a 'ghost.' This means her disembodied spirit was still attached to the memories of her life experience on Earth, and she hadn't transitioned into the spiritual world. Bree was stuck between this life and the next one. The more Bree moved forward into the spiritual realm; it became increasingly difficult to receive messages from her. When Bree completed her journey into the next plane, I quit having these visions or dreams altogether."

"Yeah, right."

"I know this is complicated and hard to take seriously. If you have additional questions later on, here's my number." Ally concluded forthrightly, writing down her name and number on a sticky note, and handing it to Elizabeth. The girl reluctantly unfolded her arms and took the slip.

"Well, at least you talked to me," Elizabeth said ungraciously.

"I'm glad we met. I sincerely hope that you can find your sister. I know Neal's been persistently looking for any possible leads." I've got to leave now to pick up my daughter from her swimming lesson, but please call if I can help you in any way." Ally got up to take her leave.

Elizabeth watched Ally leave before she got up to exit. What kind of game was this woman playing? What was her pay off? Maybe at the time, Alyssa Sullivan wanted to set up a store-front psychic shop. Maybe she runs a hotline? Elizabeth thought skeptically, and now, the woman denies any such abilities. Maybe she simply didn't want to get caught up in the lies. What difference did it make? Alyssa Sullivan and this psychic nonsense weren't going to bring her any answers about Tabitha. Elizabeth had to contemplate her next move.

When Elizabeth arrived at Marion's house, there was a note from Klay. He wanted an update; he was over at Jeannie's house. She called Klay and he came over in less than ten minutes.

"Okay give, what's up?" Klay said as he seated himself on the front stoop.

"I found out what the big secret was! You know the cover-up? What a Joke!

"What?"

"The woman -Alyssa Sullivan was posing as a psychic. Feeding your father scraps of details about the crimes."

"Are you sure?"

"I got it straight from the horse's mouth and your father was in the room. He didn't contradict anything."

"Okay?"

"You know what I think happened? The way I figure it: The woman was setting up a sham of a psychic business. You know; going through the people's trash or doing a hack job on some computer files. Somehow, she landed some information about these murders and went to check it out. The Sullivan woman and her husband found a skeleton. They decided to use it to their advantage; make a name for herself so they could really rake in the dough. This woman's credibility as a professional psychic would be established by her involvement in a murder investigation."

"Is this woman in business as a psychic now?"

"I don't think so but hear me out. The woman had to play it down, you know low-key so the cops would continue to talk to her. She even goes to work for the cops. Then, the Killer gets wise to the Sullivan woman as a player, and he goes after her. She decides the sham is much too hot to pursue and drops it. Suddenly, the Sullivan woman claims this psychic ability was fleeting, and she has lost the connection."

"I don't know. You don't know my Dad. He isn't that gullible."

"I don't know how she managed to con your father. Probably with some well-rehearsed hype. You know the kind; 'I see a body in the middle of a grassy meadow, looks like there are wooden structures nearby.' If she had found the Killer's journal or notes, she could have supplied all kinds of juicy details."

"I still think you're grossly underestimating my Dad. I don't know if he honestly believes in all this psychic jazz or not. But, if this woman was talking about visions and such; he may have hired her to keep this psychic business under wraps until the trial was over. It sounds like he didn't want any bad publicity to effect the outcome of the case. Also, whatever information this woman had, it obviously panned out; no matter where it came from originally. It was a wise move on my Dad's behalf, to make the most of the situation."

"Alright, that could be his way of thinking. He may not have wanted to confront her or fire up the situation with Sullivan afterwards. However, you were right when you said that this information wasn't likely to lead me any closer to Tabitha. I'll have to take another approach."

"I'm glad you see it my way. ....I've got to take off now. I've got an appointment this afternoon with my college advisor. I'll see you later."

Elizabeth went inside the house and logged onto her laptop. As she stared down at the keyboard, she knew what she had to do, but it was perhaps the stupidest thing she had yet contemplated. The very thought of it may her tremble in her uneasiness, but she knew she was going through with this reckless plan anyway.   It was the only course of action that she could come up with to keep up the pace in finding any answers about Tabitha.

After a brief web search, Elizabeth was on the website for the California Department of Rehabilitation and Corrections or the CDCR. The website offered a list of California prisons, and one could enter an inmate's name and find out the prison where an inmate was incarcerated. Elizabeth wrote down Eric Morrison's prison identification number and the address of Valley Correctional Center. She read the procedures on how to visit an inmate. The prisoner would have to make a request and sent an application for visitation to her. After filing out an application, the approval process could take from 2 weeks to three months. She read the twenty-five page document that outlined the way a visit was conducted from what she could bring with her, how to dress, etc. How in the world would she get approval from the board of prisons, let alone Morrison, to agree to meet with her? What kind of story could she lay out that would get her through the doors?

That's it! Thought Elizabeth with excitement. She logged into her college financial aid application. Yes, she was eligible for a Pell grant and several other awards. The transcripts of her college courses were in the car. She was all set.

Elizabeth headed to the city to register for college at Acacia State College. "I hope I don't run into Klay. The less he knows about what's going on, the better. I don't want his father-Bryant to be the wiser and throw a wrench into the works." Elizabeth silently ruminated, hoping that she'd be accepted into the college soon. She met their eligibility requirements. But just in case, she signed up and paid for a continuing education class, a short course in criminal justice. The class met once a week for a total of six weeks, and it started next week.

At the college library, Elizabeth composed her carefully worded letter to the Creep, because, she didn't want this deception to get her expelled from college before she even started. Also, she'd have to fan Morrison's ego to get him to accept and agree to her visit.

Dear Mr. Morrison,

I am a student, majoring in Criminal Justice and Criminology, enrolled at Acacia State College. Currently, I'm working on a personal project: a proposal to improve the quality of treatment programs for inmates. I've read about your criminal case in Calaveras County. I would like to hear your story. Also, I would value your opinion on any therapeutic programs you've participated in.

I hope you will be open to meeting with me. Could you please sign a visitation application and list me as a friend since this proposal is part of my independent studies. Then, send the application to me so I can fill in my information. You will have to let me know when it's approved. Then, I will be able to visit and talk to you about this important project.

I will deposit $15 into your inmate account to cover the cost of any postage.

Thank You,

Elizabeth Lenard

Elizabeth hoped that the Creep would respond. Would he recognize her surname? No, she didn't think so. She also knew that most prisoners usually welcomed any visitor; just as a break from the monotony and boredom of prison life. She'd learned that from her Mom. Meanwhile, she would pick up a money order for $15 and have it deposited into Morrison's inmate account. But after that, she would just have to wait.

Eric read the letter from Elizabeth Lenard again, short and sweet. Another bored and sheltered debutante, who wants to meet the big, bad wolf. Probably, believes she can psychoanalyze him. He'd enjoy playing her! How much money could he eventually get out of her to put into his commissary account? Depending on how gullible or needy, he could put this one to good use, down the line. He'd love to get off a few messages to the family, and especially, to the Sullivan Bitch. The Bitch probably figures by now he'd forgotten all about her. She'll have completely relaxed her guard. And boom! Then, the message would arrive. His note would create havoc and fear all over again. She wouldn't be able to let that maggot of hers' out of her sight. Just part of the pay back; which is long overdue. He'd been laxly planning her death for too long; it would feel great to take some concrete action.

He sat in front of his notebook and formulated his response. His reply needed to be articulate, but not too elaborate. He didn't want to spook this little socialite. Just enough, to start reeling her in, and get a fix on her. Okay.

Dear Ms. Lenard,

I received your courteous request for information. I would be happy to assist you in your educational study. I believe much can be gained from correctly diagnosing maladaptive behaviors and offering early interventions and high-quality treatment. I only wish that I had received such effective therapy, when I was younger. Then possibly, the resulting tragedies could have been averted.

Sadly and to my own detriment, I acknowledge my culpability in the deaths of those young, innocent children. However in my case, I also, ascribe blame to the juvenile welfare system. The problems I had as a child, were clearly evident, and placed me at substantial risk for an aberrant or a destructive response. In other words, I needed extensive help and support, which I failed to receive. Ultimately, my abysmal reaction to my unfortunate upbringing; in concert with the dereliction of attention and care by a governmental agency, resulted in a needless catastrophe. It pains me to realize what part I played in the resulting calamity.

Now with some psychological insight, I understand the victims; those beautiful girls, also needed a great deal of help and support, which they woefully didn't receive. These troubled children had suffered, just as I had, from abuse and neglect. Many delinquent behaviors are often rooted in child abuse, domestic violence, substance abuse, or mental illness. Likewise, many victims of violence have suffered from similar circumstances; the fate of having an unhealthy childhood. Our society seems unable to address these problems systematically, resulting in an inadequate response to criminal conduct. We penalize criminal behavior but do not adequately treat the root causes of crime.

I hope you understand my position. Proper research and educational studies may lead to holistic programs, which inclusively link causes of behavior with criminal conduct. Then, these interventions must have adequate funding and full implementation to have a significant impact on our social and criminal justice systems. I hope your educational study isn't short sighted but injects a full long range vision.

I've enclosed a signed visitation form. I look forward to meeting with you.

Sincerely,

Eric Morrison

The following week, Elizabeth received the letter from Morrison. He was a bigger tool then she thought, a real loser. Elizabeth couldn't believe how pathetic this Creep was. She felt 'the system' sucked too, but she didn't blame it for all of her fuck-ups! How rich! Who was he to lecture about compassion and empathy? He believed she was going to suck up all this crap. How was she going to work this Creep without giving herself away?

Ally put Breanna down for her nap and started to prepare for her busy afternoon. First, she should catch up on her case notes, but Ally couldn't focus on her task. She leaned back her head, closed her eyes, and started rubbing her temples, in an attempt to relax.

Ally must have drifted off to sleep. In the daydream, the scene that she was viewing was through a man's eyes -not her own. From a distance, he watched the door to an apartment and then scrutinized the notebook page in front of him. The name: "Brooke Hubbard," was written in a strong, forceful print along with other identity information such as birthdate and address. He flipped back a couple of pages in the notebook to stare intently at a photo that was paper clipped to the interior side of the notebook cover. The image was of a young girl.

The youngster, in the photo, twinkling a 'toothless' grin for the camera. Both of her front baby teeth were missing; she must have recently lost them. The precious child had a sparkle of merriment in her bright, blue eyes, her abundantly freckled face and bright red hair seemed to emanate a lively, outgoing, and cheerful disposition. "A little firecracker" was the descriptive in Ally's mind.

The man's eyes suddenly darted back to the door of Apartment 2C. A small child skipped jubilantly, her backpack bouncing up and down with her free-spirited movements. She pulled up a key from the neckline of her colorful tee-shirt; it was attached to a long chain around her neck. She opened the locked door of the apartment and went inside, closing the door behind her.

Ally saw the man reach down and open the car door. He got out of the car, quickly shutting the door behind him without a glance. His focus remained fixed on the door. He headed in a rush, towards the apartment door. He knocked briskly, but no one answered. He knocked louder and more vigorously but no response. He persistently continued to knock; then, his ear was pressed against the door listening for any activity. No sound was evident. The man walked around the apartment complex and strained himself upward, attempting to peer through the back, glass sliding door. He couldn't see anything but the edge of the kitchen counter.

He continued to stare at the exterior of the apartment, looking at windows, and pulling at the back wooden gate. His hand reached over the gate to feel for a latch or lock. He was looking for a way in, Ally concluded. He took several steps back staring once again at the exterior of the complex before he turned away.

Ally's eyes shot open. Oh my god! What was that? She hadn't had any psychic visions in over three years. Little Bree had been channeling them. Once Bree had moved on to the spirit world, the visions had ceased. If Bree was no longer able to transmit any visual imagery to her, from where did this dream originate? Who was this child, Brooke Hubbard?   Was she another victim? Oh dear God, could Brooke now be sending her visions? Or could it be Tabitha? Was the spirit of another dead child trying to contact her?

Ally had to talk to Neal.   Ally ran to the phone to call.

"Neal, this is Ally."

"Hi Ally," Neal started but she quickly interrupted him.

"Oh God, Neal, I've just had a vision. This psychic thing, it has started again."

"Okay Ally, slow down and tell me about your dream."

"Neal, this one was different. Much more alarming! It was as if I saw the scene first-person through Eric's eyes. I didn't become 'Eric' but I could see what he was doing as if I were him. ....How do I explain this element? I was still myself with my own perspective.

"I understand."

"Eric was stalking a little girl. I believe her name was Brooke Hubbard; he had her photo, name, and address in his notebook. The little girl had to be six or seven years old because Brooke was missing her two front baby teeth in the photo. The child had red hair, blue eyes, and freckles.

Brooke arrived at the apartment and let herself inside. Eric went to the door and repeatedly knocked. No one answered: the child must have been told not to answer the door when no one else was home. Then, Eric went around the back of the apartment complex. He was looking for a way inside. He seemed to have given up and was about to leave, when I awoke.

"That's good, Ally. I can follow up on your vision and see if I can find any record of Brooke Hubbard ever living in Calaveras County. I'll let you know what I find."

"Thank you, Neal. Please let me know what you find out."

"Creep!" Silently, Elizabeth stared at the man in front of her with her best yet, poker face. Funny, you'd never know by just looking that this guy is a twisted fuck-up.

Disguising her contempt, Elizabeth tried to act like one of her social workers. "I appreciate the comments in your letter about treatment needs. I understand that any therapeutic interventions need to be comprehensive and multi-leveled. The goal of my project proposal is to correlate specific therapies to the particular crimes committed. Therefore, I would first like to overview your crimes for case documentation purposes.

Eric stared back; he was perplexed by her response. Most people he encountered had a morbid curiosity about the crimes but were reluctant to discuss them. Similar to driving past a gruesome auto accident, most people are compelled to look but are afraid of what they might see. This girl jumped right in without even trying to brag up her project or attempt to show off her intellectual proclivities.

Elizabeth consults notes: "First, I have questions as to why you left all your victims near that mining camp. You know the Animas Mine. Did the location have any special meaning for you?

"When I was about nine years old, I had a friend whose father was a mining engineer. This guy took me and his son to the mine several times. He told us about mining stuff and even showed us some of the equipment and how it was used. I guess the memory of the place stuck."

Oh, there he goes trying to suck me into his sob story. Don't roll your eyes, you need him to keep talking. She jotted down some nonsense about the nostalgia of his childhood experience. "Okay, my second question; the child victims were about the same age, six or seven years old. Why do you think you choose victims from that age group?"

"I helped my sister to run-away from home when she was six years old. She was okay, but the childhood experience was very traumatizing for me. I was never allowed to return home to my family again. I believe that somehow I was reliving this experience in my mind. Probably some kind of post traumatic experience or flashback." Elizabeth jotted down: psychological trauma from a childhood event.

"How many children did you victimize?"

"Four, I thought you told me that you'd reviewed the criminal investigation?" Eric tried to gage her reaction as he contemplated whether or not she could be secretly working for the asshole -Bryant.

"I saw a segment on a news program about your case that indicated there may have been additional victims."

"Before I answer your question, I have a favor to ask of you, first.   I'm trying to make amends slowly for my past actions. During the investigation, I hurt a nice lady, Alyssa Sullivan. I was out of my mind at the time and often, had black-outs, gaps of time that I cannot even remember. I would like to apologize for damage I did. Later when I work up the courage, I'd like to talk to the families of my other victims but that is still too difficult. I hope you can deliver an apology note to Ms. Sullivan. She lives in Maplewood, and she's in the phonebook. I'm afraid that the prison might not send out the letter because of her victim status. He slipped her a sealed envelope in the back of her notebook.

"Okay. Now, back to your case history: How many victims were there? Are there any victims that aren't accounted for?" Elizabeth asked, a little too intently.

"You read the investigation."

"I wanted to verify the facts."

"You were put up to this by Bryant."

"Who are you talking about?" Elizabeth responded and Eric lifted his eyebrows sardonically.

"I want to know what happened to this little girl. A photo of her was in your trailer!" She held out a picture of Tabitha. Elizabeth had blown her ploy, so she took a direct approach.

"What's it to you?" Eric said, leaning back casually.

"She's my sister, you filthy, piece of shit!"

"I'm not saying anymore."

"Of course, you're not. You stupid loser. Do you really think I was buying your line of crap?"

Menacing, Eric roughly grabbed her arm. Elizabeth responded automatically with a sharp right cross to his jaw, momentarily blind-sighting him; Eric toppled off the bench.

"Shit, you fuckin' Bitch!" Eric shouted as he got to his feet.

"The guards rushed over to separate them, leading Elizabeth away and out of the visitation room. Elizabeth said innocently; he tried to hurt me, so I had to defend myself. She could hear the buzzer in the background as another guard announced the visits were concluded for the day.

Once she was outside the prison gate, Elizabeth realized that she had the sealed envelope for Alyssa Sullivan. Elizabeth quickly opened the Envelope and read:

You'll get yours, Bitch! It's just a matter of time. I'm still dreaming about what I'm going to do to your daughter before I kill her. I'm never going to quit until you're both dead!

Elizabeth walked back to the prison gate and rang the bell. She asked to talk to a duty sergeant.

When the guard appeared, Elizabeth said, "Eric Morrison slipped this letter into my notebook. He asked me to deliver it to a woman, Alyssa Sullivan, who lives in Maplewood. When I told him that I couldn't deliver any letter, he became violent. He viciously grabbed my arm and threatened me. That is why I had to defend myself by slugging him. Here's the letter that he handed me." She said, then walked away.

Alyssa Sullivan wasn't a partner in the crimes; that's for sure. Elizabeth didn't think there was ever a liaison between the two of them or the 'threat' would have been more personalized. The Sullivan woman must have scored the information by other means, just as Elizabeth surmised.

Neal Bryant came home in an irascible mood and demanded to speak to Klay, alone.

Once they got to the living room, Neal unleashed the tirade. "What were you thinking Klay? Why didn't you tell me that Elizabeth was going to see Morrison at the prison?"

"What?" Klay said, dumbfounded.

"She could've been seriously hurt! It was a fool-hearty gesture, which could have got her, and others hurt in the ensuing fiasco. She met with him in loosely supervised setting, and it wasn't even behind protective glass."

"Honestly Dad, I don't know what you're talking about."

"I'm sorry, Klay. It obvious that you don't know what the hell is going on. I thought you must have known what Elizabeth was planning to do, since she claimed to be a criminology major at your school. ...Elizabeth used a ruse to con Morrison into signing a visitation form for her. She claimed to be working on an independent research project but instead went into the prison to confront Morrison on her sister's whereabouts."

"She did what?"

"Morrison caught on and grabbed her in a threatening manner. She decked him, knocked him to the ground." Neal said, stifling a small grin. "I got called on the carpet and had to answer to charges made by Morrison. He claimed I put this girl up to this: an undercover operation to set him up. I had to make sense of what happened and then, explain this outlandish situation, since my name was dragged into it. I don't think anyone believes I was involved, but I don't want my credibility hurt in the legal community."

"I'm sorry; you got caught up in this mess. I would have given you a head-up about her plans if I had known."

CHAPTER 5

"It was a bust!" The encounter with the Creep hadn't brought her any closer to finding Tabitha. Again, Elizabeth was at a standstill. What would she do now? It was time to regroup. She needed to retrace her steps from the beginning. She might have missed something along the way. Elizabeth gathered the video tape of the *"Mystery Source"* segment, the legal brief by Weiss, and the letter from the Creep. She popped the VHS in the player; then, proceeded to sit down along with her notebook with pen in hand.

For the first time, Elizabeth noted the older photo of the Eric Morrison on the pre-recorded program. Initially, when she'd watched this segment, her mind had been focused on Tabitha. She hadn't noticed the Creep. Morrison had what her brother, Sammy would have termed a 'preppie' look. I guess the adult version of a preppie, would be that of a 'yuppie' appearance. He looked urbane, affluent, attractive, and spoilt, like he had more money than common sense. During her meeting with Morrison, Elizabeth knew the Creep was a disgusting worm but he bore an air of 'respectability.' He still maintained that mixture of arrogance, civility, and composure; as if he was condescendingly looking down his nose at her, while HE conducted the interview.

Elizabeth reread the letter that man had sent to her. Again, the Creep held the mannerisms of an arrogant and self-righteous hypocrite as she read between the lines and dissected his message. He seemed to take responsibility for killing those children but quickly turned it into all that shit about the failure of the system. He placed the blame of his fuck-ups on upbringing, the system, society, and even on the victims –themselves. As though, if those children didn't have such a pathetic environment, they wouldn't have been targeted in the first place. Moreover, he implied that if you have a lousy childhood, you become either a perp or a victim. Yeah right, what about me? I didn't have the greatest childhood either, but I'm neither, a killer or a victim.

According to this Creep's philosophy, if you didn't have a shoddy upbringing, that made you a 'clueless' outsider. As an outsider, you didn't care or couldn't be bothered with the dire circumstances of others. You pigeon-holed "others" into an undesirable class below your scope and vision; a class, which did not merit support or help. An outsider meads out ineffective services, more intent on penalizing rather than helping others. Elizabeth felt that the system often fell short, but most people were motivated by good intentions. Her views weren't as sorry as that Creep's!

Elizabeth wondered what Klay's take on Eric Morrison and this letter would be. It's funny; she hadn't heard from him in several days. He was probably busy getting his college schedule situated. She reviewed Weiss' brief and her notes. She couldn't find any loose facts to investigate. She should contact this news program, and see if they were willing to do an update on the situation. Maybe putting Tabitha's story out there nationally, could yield some results?

Klay missed Elizabeth! But, he felt he was wasting his time and energy in pursuing anything deeper. The relationship wasn't going anywhere. Klay had felt that Elizabeth's attention was solely centered on finding her sister in a single-minded fashion, but it was more than these unfortunate circumstances. She was determined to keep herself at an emotional distance because she feared the intimacy of a close relationship. Klay didn't believe that she was ever going to open up to him or to anyone else for that matter.

And what about that Morrison situation? He couldn't believe she hadn't leveled with him and told him what she was planning to do. The girl was totally self-absorbed! She didn't care about how her actions affected anyone else. And he was more than tired of playing the middle man between Elizabeth and his father. He didn't sign on for that role!

The more Klay contemplated his relationship with Elizabeth, he realized he couldn't leave her in the lurch. It wasn't fair! He had to get real and discuss his feelings with her. Give Elizabeth a choice on whether their relationship continued or not. He had to make a strong point that the relationship couldn't continue on its' present course. He wasn't going to be her lap dog; only there when she needed him, but then quickly cast aside. Klay needed Elizabeth to take their relationship as seriously as he did.

"Solitary confinement." Eric Morrison sat in the isolated, stark white cell behind the windowless, solid-metal door. A horizontal, vented window on the far wall, provided very little in the way of natural light and gave a compressed view of the outside courtyard. His restless thoughts were the only occupants of this barren void.

That little she-wolf had bested him! He didn't see it coming; Eric thought dangerously, while absently rubbing his sore jaw. He got up and agitatedly started pacing back and forth within the cramped confines of the cell. Elizabeth Lenard was certainly no debutante or socialite, just dirty trailer trash! She certainly had no reservations about suckering him. Eric started to slam a fist repeatedly into his opposing hand, as the frantic rhythm of his pacing increased in unleashed fury. But, it was going to be hard to get at her in any typical fashion. The problem was that trashy, bar-room brawler wasn't afraid of him. She was all too eager to corporally mix it up with him; to give him as much fight, as she got. ...Despite her brash crudity, he had to admit the tramp had a brain. The conniving shrew had deviously duped him into that visit, manipulated the encounter, and seized control. Finally, she set him up with that message, which she turned over to the guards. Because of her disclosure, he'd been sent to solitary for issuing terrorist threats, and thus, he was stuck in isolation for ten days.

Yes, the vicious tramp was far too rash and unpredictable. He had to bring on his best game to out play her. The one card that he could play, which would give him the upper hand, was his knowledge about her sister, his lost discard. He had to use this ammunition; leverage it to his advantage.

First, he had to get out of this rat trap; escape from this fucking institution! He had wasted too much time here already. Then, old debts needed to be settled. An image of the Bitch -Ally flashed in his mind, as he ran his tongue across his lips. The Bitch with the clinging, maggot pod were his prime obsession. As such, images of their gruesome demise persistently hovered within the backdrop of his waking thoughts for almost four years now. Currently, they were unreachable targets, living on HIS borrowed time, because he was rotting in this cage. As he felt the pressure mount; he knew it was time to take action.

Neal knew he should call Ally, but he was reluctant. He probably should inform her about Morrison's threats against her and Breanna. But, he didn't want to open up all those old wounds again. Did these threats really matter anyway? Morrison was behind bars to stay. He owed Ally a call anyway, because he had some background information about Brooke Hubbard.

Okay. He picked up the phone to call Ally. His relief was evident, when the call went straight through to her voice mail. He left the following message: Hi Ally; it's Neal. I found some information about Brooke Hubbard. Give me a call, and I'll give you an update. Talk to you later.

Ally returned Neal's call in the early afternoon. "Hi Neal, you have information about the child that I dreamt about?"

"Yes, I found a record of Brooke Hubbard, a seven-year-old girl. The child attended the second grade at Pendleton Elementary in 1992."

"Where you able to contact her or the family?"

"Not yet. The girl moved out of the area with her mother that same year."

"Oh dear God no, Neal!" Ally said in exasperation. "Everyone thought that Amy George and Priscilla McCabe had moved away, but they were dead the whole time."

"Whoa, Ally! I know the timing of the relocation of this family is suspicious, given your insights. However, we cannot jump to any conclusion until we verify the facts."

"Couldn't Pendleton school secretary tell you which school Brooke's records were transferred to?"

"It's complicated!"

"What's complicated about a simple question, like this one?

Neal took a deep breath and exhaled slowly. Then he replied slowly, "I'll give you the background information about Brooke. The child's father, Vince Hubbard, died in a motorcycle accident when Brooke was an infant. Her mother, Lana Silvers remarried in the late 1980's; her new spouse was extremely abusive. There were numerous domestic violence reports from the home. Eventually, Lana Silvers was able to break away and leave her husband, but he kept harassing her. He swore that he'd kill her and her daughter. Ms. Silver pursued a restraining order against the estranged husband, Daniel Silvers, but he continued to violate the court order. Ms. Silvers, fearing for the safety of herself and her girl, left the area. The mother picked up Brooke's school records prior to the move. She didn't want to leave any official records or tell anyone where she was moving to, due to fear that her ex would find them. I've been trying to locate Lana Silver, but haven't had any luck so far."

"I guess we're waiting for any leads on her contact information?"

"I could track her down through her social security number or her DMV records. However, I need a court order to obtain her information because she's requested that her records remain confidential. Smart move on her part, given the circumstances. Currently, I don't have any foundation for requesting this information. I've contacted several distant relatives and known associates to see if they can get a message to her, asking for her to contact me."

"I'm waiting for a response. If I don't hear something soon, I'll write a letter. I'll explain that her daughter's name came up in the context of this investigation; I want to verify the safety and well-being of Brooke Hubbard. I believe this request will elicit a response. If all is kosher, she'll want to know why our office was concerned about her daughter's welfare."

"I certainly would want to know what was going on. Thanks, Neal, I appreciate the update."

"Ally, I've got something else to tell you, but I don't want you to get too worked up about it."

"What is it?" Ally inquired with concern.

"Long story, but Elizabeth Lenard conned her way into the prison to meet with Morrison."

"Oh, Good Lord!" Is she okay?"

"Yes, she even managed to give him a good right hook before she was hauled away! "

"Umm...okay?"

"At first, Morrison thought she was a regular college student, working on a research project. He tried to get her to deliver a message to you. Ms. Lenard gave this note to the guard. It was a death threat against you and Breanna."

"Is that all? I don't see why you're so concerned about it. Of course, he seized the opportunity to try to rile me up and frighten me. He can't hurt me from prison."

"I'm glad to see that you're not upset about the threat."

"No, not at all."

"I'll give you a call, when I find out more about Brooke."

"Thanks, I hope you hear something soon. I'll talk to you, later," Ally concluded the call.

Klay drove over to Marion's house, reflecting on, in fact, rehearsing what he wanted to say to Elizabeth. The girl valued her independence and freedom. He knew he had to tread carefully, or she would tell him to 'get lost' without so much as a second thought. From what Klay had learned about Elizabeth's past, she had only herself to depend on. Self-reliance was the cornerstone of her foundation. Trust wouldn't come easily to her since she'd been let down many times before throughout her childhood. He could be viewed as a threat to her established boundaries, which she viewed as essential for her own survival. Somehow, Klay had to convince Elizabeth that he was a valuable ally and a source of unwavering support. Someone, she could count on.

Gravely, Klay knocked on the door. Elizabeth looked surprised to see him as she answered the door. "Hi Elizabeth."

"How have you been? Did you get your classes squared away?" Elizabeth inquired.

"Yes, I got the classes I needed. ...Elizabeth, we need to talk."

Oh God, here it comes, thought Elizabeth, taking in Klay's grim demeanor. She hated these good-bye spiels! She was no good at them at all. It was best to get it done and over with quickly.

"About what?" came Elizabeth's curt and uncompromising reply.

"There is something I want you to think about and consider regarding our relationship."

"What relationship?" Elizabeth said condescendingly.

"My point exactly," Klay said succinctly, noting Elizabeth's baffled expression.

"I care for you and want our relationship to develop. I don't want it to be a mere friendly association, remaining stagnant and superficial. I want to be there for you all the time, not just when you need me. I want you to open up and have confidence in me. Trust me to be there for you."

"You're always coming over here whenever you want to, even when I haven't wanted to talk."

"I shouldn't have to insist that we talk. You really should want to confine in me because you feel the need to share. Moreover, I want to be able to talk to you about anything and everything without the fear of chasing you away. Mutually, I want you to be there for me. A relationship is always a two-way street, if it's a healthy one.

"I'm not ready to commit to you or anyone else. I need to get an education and figure out what I want to do in the future. I don't even have a clue about what career to pursue."

"I'm not asking you to commit yourself to me fully right now. Just to open up, and see if a deeper relationship is possible. Let yourself consider the possibility. Whether or not we're meant to be together forever, I don't know. This is something we both need to look at and take seriously when the time comes. Even if our relationship doesn't end up in marriage, I believe we could have a deep and lasting friendship.

"We're already friends," Elizabeth said on the defensive.

"That's a cop out and you know it. I would like our relationship to become deeper, more intimate. That won't happen unless you're willing to open up to me and let down some of your defenses.

"Jump into bed with you, you mean!"

"I said nothing about sex. This is about emotional, not physical intimacy, being there for each other. Not just me being available for you if you need something. I'm not going to be used that way!"

"Yeah right."

"I'll give you time to think about what I've said and make your decision. I really do want to be with you, Elizabeth. I'll come back by in a few days and see what you've decided." Klay turned around and left.

"The nerve of that guy, who did he think he was anyway!" Elizabeth fumed in frustration. She'd known him for a matter of weeks, and here he was already making demands.

David awoke at 4:30 in the morning; because, he had an early delivery at Smart Grocery store, where he was the manager. After her husband had left the house, Ally fell back into a disturbed sleep. Her nonsensical dream waned as a new clairvoyant vision materialized.

Again, Ally was viewing the scene through the man –Eric Morrison's eyes. This time, Eric wasn't parked outside Brooke's apartment. He was following the child in his car as the young girl merrily pranced down a desolate street. It seemed as if the child was on her way home from school because her backpack was slung carelessly over one shoulder while she swung her plastic lunchbox in stride.

Brooke became alert to the foreboding danger; aware of the fact that she was being watched. Her merriment subsided, and her harried movements became markedly more distressed. Nervously, the child darted several, wary glances over her shoulder at the pursuing vehicle. In accordance, the girl's pace quickened in response to each urgent glance.

Suddenly, Brooke made a swift dash up to the front doorway of a nearby home; frantically ringing the doorbell, before charging through the unlocked door. Someone peered out from behind the closed blinds, as Eric sped away down the street. He repeatedly slammed his closed fist into the steering wheel in frustration.

Ally awoke with her heart pounding in double time; the adrenaline pumping throughout her body. Her anxiety, heightened by fear for this child -Brooke. Ally kept reminding herself that these were historical events that took place over ten years ago. She couldn't alter any circumstances of these elapsed episodes.

Ally cogitated; Eric had been trailing Brooke after her school day ended. Most likely, this was the only time that the child was left on her own. Why didn't Lana Silvers hire a babysitter to look after her daughter? Then Ally realized, the mother probably couldn't afford daycare. At the time, Lana was leaving an abusive marriage. Unfortunately, it wasn't likely that she had any adequate, financial resources. Lana and her daughter probably just made it out of the marital home with the clothes on their backs!

Ally shuttered at her own ominous thoughts. Did Eric manage to track down Brooke? Ally wondered what horrors the poor child faced. Would she, herself, be subjected to a first-person account of Eric's depravity? Oh God! Would she have to witness Brooke's death before these visions finally ceased?

Frantically, Ally was propelled towards the kitchen to call Neal. Hopefully, he had some luck in finding Lana Silvers. Ally was driven by her frantic need for answers regarding Brooke before she went crazy, considering all the adverse conclusions!

Elizabeth hadn't seen Klay for over three days. Damn, if she didn't miss his company! He always managed to give her a differing perspective on situations that arose. His insights were generally practical and made overall sense. Marion was due to return home from her sister's place at the end of the week. The woman had offered to let her stay on at the house until she moved into the dorms at the end of August. Even though, Elizabeth was considering this proposition. She felt it might be better to move away from the area because of Klay and his family. She'd have to think about it. She couldn't afford to be too noble!

Elizabeth probably would have taken off already, but she was waiting for a response from that newsmagazine. She had left an e-mail message for the producers of 'Mystery Source.' She still hadn't received any word about her request for them to do a segment on Tabitha. However, she was certain that they receive multitudes of these types of requests. Hers was likely buried among all the other letters.

Oh no, for crying out loud! She dreaded the thought that just struck her. Bryant had solicited the initial story with this news program regarding the possibility of an unknown victim of Morrison – that Creep. Bryant obviously knew the right people to contact at 'Mystery Source.' He had an 'in' with the program executives. Maybe she'd have to play nice with Bryant and get him to make an official request.

Elizabeth really could use Klay's help right now with this negotiation. He said that he wanted a deeper friendship. She had to approach either Klay or his father to expedite the communication process with 'Mystery Source.' Right now, she didn't know which one was more formidable. She would just have to bite the bullet and call Klay. It was so humiliating to have to ask for his help at this juncture. But, she didn't believe Bryant would go out of his way to help her. Okay, she might as well get it done and over with by making the call. Despite their tiff, Elizabeth didn't think Klay would refuse to help her. He just wasn't like that.

His first day out of solitary confinement, and Eric sat in the rec room watching a ho-hum talk show on daytime television. In the show, two adult daughters refused to reconcile with their despondent mother, who had been diagnosed with Cancer. The female hostess asked each of the daughters if they couldn't forgive their mother's past mistakes because they may not get a chance to make amends in the future. Their mother's prognosis for the Cancer appeared unpromising. Both bitches refused to reconsider their self-righteous position.

At least, this mother was begging for a relationship with her children despite the bitchy attitudes of her kids. He hadn't seen or heard from his fucking mother in over three years. 'Mother dearest' had made only one appearance at the prison. Her ulterior motive for the visit was to plead with him not to go on a news show and 'discuss their personal family business.' Ha! Is that what she called it? He called it child sexual abuse and neglect, as well as childhood emotional devastation. Mother always did have a way of skirting past the dirtiest issues.

Eric would lay odds that little she-wolf didn't have a mother either. That tramp, Elizabeth was much too wild and impulsive. She'd never been taught to be 'polite, behave nicely, and play well with others.' He still had to come up with something real special to level the playing field with her. Uncomfortably, he deliberated, it wouldn't be easy! Not like it would be, playing with the Bitch, Ally; she was almost too easy and predictable. He could come up with a hundred lures and ruses to reel the Bitch in, her and that maggot child. Use her 'little Mother Teresa saving the children' act against her. Maybe he could start by kidnapping her maggot child, and get the dumb Bitch to come alone after the pod.

Eric replayed one of his frequent fantasies involving the Bitch. As Eric visualized the Bitch's bloody corpse with her mangled, detached limbs mingled with that of the Maggot, Eric felt the carnal response of his body to the imagery. He made his way to his cell in order to master his physical arousal.

Afterward, Eric reclined on his cot and ruminated. Yes! He had to escape from this rat trap. He started to formulate his escape plan. This plan had to be fool-proof because he couldn't afford to fail. Certainly, it would be simpler to escape from the hospital wing than any place else in the prison. Occasionally, he still had seizures from a beating he got in prison years ago. He'd have to fake a seizure that wouldn't be too tough. Now, to devise and orchestrate each step towards his freedom.

Ally was putting Breanna down for a nap when the phone rang. She rushed to her bedroom to answer the call, "Hello."

"Hi Ally;" it was Neal. "I'm hoping that you could come in today at 2:30?"

"Yes, of course, I can. I'll make arrangemenst to drop Breanna off at her preschool this afternoon. What's up?"

"I've got a surprise for you! I'll explain everything when you get here."

"I'll see you at 2:30, then." Ally hung up the receiver, wondering what was happening now. She better get ready to go.

"Hi Karen," Ally said as she approached the reception desk. "Neal is expecting me, can I go back to his office?"

"Great to see you, Ally. Yes, you can go on back. Neal is waiting for you," she said with a smile.

When Ally opened the door to Neal's office, she saw that Neal wasn't alone. A vaguely familiar, young woman with auburn hair and blue eyes, was sitting across from him at the desk. "Hello?"

Neal stood up as Ally entered the room. "Hi Ally, I'd like you to meet someone. This is Brooke 'Hubbard' Feland. Brooke, this is Alyssa Sullivan."

Ally was aghast, looking wide-eyed at the teen. Ally attempted to quell her own hand from quivering as she greeted Brooke with a handshake.

"Hi?" Brooke said with a questioning smile, as she noticed Alyssa Sullivan's strange reaction to her presence.

"Brooke Feland, just arrived. Her cousin -Toni, contacted Ms. Feland, here, and told her that we wanted to talk to her in connection to a murder investigation.   She was naturally alarmed, but I explained that she wasn't in any trouble. We just wanted to talk to her."

Ally nodded at the girl, "You can call me, Ally. May I call you, Brooke?"

"Yes. ...Could you please tell me what's going on?" Brooke asked in bewilderment, visibly growing more anxious.

"Brooke, how old are you? Maybe you want your mother to be here?"

"I'm eighteen now, and I want to know what's going on! I'll fill my Mom in, later.

"Alright. It's complicated," Neal began. "In 1998, I arrested Eric Morrison for the murder of four little girls; he is currently in prison for these crimes. Our department believed there was another victim by this killer, but he wouldn't give us any more information. "

"Okay, but what does this matter, have to do with me?" Brooke inquired.

"Recently, we learned that Morrison could have targeted you as a victim.   This killer was skilled at hiding any trail of his victims. You left the county in 1992 at the age of seven; the same age as Morrison's other victims. And you seemed to disappear without a trace. Our office wanted to be sure that you were safe," Neal finished.

"I knew it wasn't Dan! My stepfather threatened to kill my mom and me. I told my mom that some man followed me home from school. Another time, this same guy kept knocking at the door of our apartment, but I knew better then to answer the door. I did tell Mom that it wasn't Dan, but she believed that he was behind it. She wasn't going to take any chances! We moved to Nevada County to stay with my grandparents. Eventually, Mom met Bob, and they married. Soon after the marriage, Bob adopted me because they both feared that Dan would try to harm Mom or me. The adoption allowed me to change my name legally. Bob, my Dad, is a great man; he's been wonderful to me."

"Well, due to some information we've obtained, I do believe that Morrison was stalking you. I'm pleased to see that your Mom was so diligent and protective. It was a real godsend that you relocated out-of-the-area when you did." Neal concluded.

"Are you telling me this move, probably saved my life? That: I narrowly escaped with my life from that serial killer?"

"Yes, I believe you did."

"Oh my God, I can't believe it."

"Yes. You are extremely lucky. I'm glad we were able to meet with you and make sure you are okay. Thank you for coming in."

As Brooke left the office, Ally deduced that the messages – these intuitive visions were not coming from Brooke. Therefore, it had to be Tabitha. Oh God, poor Elizabeth! What is she going to do when she finds out for certain that Tabitha is dead?

As Elizabeth stepped out the front door to take for a walk, she saw that Jeannie buckling Kayla into her car seat. Jeannie looked up to see Elizabeth, and quickly crossed the road in order to meet up with her.

"Hi Elizabeth, I wanted to talk to you, but I don't have too long," Jeannie said, briefly glancing at the car.

"What's up?" Elizabeth questioned.

"I know it's really none of my business. But, Klay is really a decent guy, besides being my brother. I don't want him to get hurt! I know he cares about you, deeply. Please, if you don't feel the same way about him, don't lead him on. That's really all I want to say!"

"I'm not trying to lead him on!"

"Please, just think about what you're doing. I've got to go now. See you around." Jeannie rejoined; then, she marched back to her car, got in, and left.

Holy hell! Elizabeth didn't get 'these' people! All Elizabeth had done, is ask Klay to intercede with his Dad on her behalf. She needed to connect with the producers of *'Mystery Source,'* and persuade the newsmagazine to do a segment on Tabitha. Was that asking too much! Tabitha had been missing for over ten years; she could be dead. No one could give her any more information. And there was Jeannie griping about her brother's feelings; accusing her of taking advantage of him. Jeannie didn't even understand what she was dealing with in regards to her sister. How would Jeannie feel if her brother was missing and no one really gave a damn?

After a few minutes, Elizabeth pondered; what were her feelings regarding Klay anyway? They were friends! She missed talking with him. He always gave her a different viewpoint, worth considering. Elizabeth also realized that at some level, she counted on Klay, which she couldn't say about very many people.

CHAPTER 6

"Brooke Hubbard;" that was the label of his second target; Eric ruminated. He had tracked his prey for weeks and was going in for the kill. The plan had been impeccable! It came with the perfect set-up, the pathetic dick of a step-father would have taken the rap. Then Abracadabra, the mark had simply disappeared; it was gone without a trace.

His plan got all fucked up; just as he was revved up for the slaughter. Eric sprang up from his cot and started manically pacing back and forth in the cramped cell. His movements became more erratic as he recalled driving away heedlessly, from the empty apartment in frustration. At the time, he was pinging out of control as he drove around restlessly but aimlessly for hours. The need, to take action, was crucial! Suddenly out of the nowhere, the police scanner gave him the answer, a replacement.

The "replicate" mark could easily be substituted into his plan. The po -po were looking for a sleazebag woman, who took off with her six-year-old sprog. The brat was taken into state custody, when the mother gave the morons the slip. Eric clutched his upper arms tightly, rocking to and fro; the frenzied pacing continued. He recalled thinking; surely that sleazebag mother would stay off the grid and take the state route out of the area. There was only one rest stop along that corridor. Quickly regrouping, he took a back road shortcut to waylay the pair.

The alternative plan had seemed priceless; because of course, that sleazy bitch of a mother wouldn't notify the authorities when her offspring disappeared. Eric visualized the memory in a cystal-clear precision. He had canvased the rest stop and laid in wait, ready for the hunt. Sure enough, the sleazebag woman stopped to use the restroom. The bitch entered the small toilet enclosure, leaving the bait unattended. He had acted quickly, clasping a hand over the mouth of his surrogate and dumped it in the back of the jeep. Despite the impetuous nature of the change-up, this new plan should have gone off without a hitch. How did such an ideal ancillary plan get so screwed up in the end? He kicked forcefully at the base of his cot.

Unfulfilled, Eric shook his head to clear out the memories; it was no good to dwell on failures. But, he had learned from that debacle. Each and every plan had to be meticulously planned out, or failure was inevitable. His escape plan was going to be flawless! He was just waiting for Al to come through for him. Then, he would set a date.

Elizabeth sat in the lawn chair with Ellie curled in her lap. Klay sat in the adjacent chair. Elizabeth agreed to give their relationship, "a go"; but told Klay she was taking it a day at a time. Now, she felt a slight weirdness whenever she was around him. But, she supposed that she was glad to have the company.

"I talked to Dad; he contacted the producers of that show, "Mystery Source." He'll call you once he receives any word, pro or con, but he believed that they would be willing to do a follow-up segment about Tabitha." Klay informed her.

"Thanks for asking for me. I'm sure your dad doesn't want to include me."

"You're wrong. On the contrary, he said a personal appeal from you could go a long ways; much better than him asking for information. Get people to personalize the story."

"I'm glad to hear it that he doesn't want to cut me out of the picture."

Klay decided to change the subject, "I read the copy of Morrison's letter that you gave me. I think you were mostly right in your assessment, regarding his perspective. But, I also thought that Morrison was telling "his truth," despite his obvious manipulations. That's how he views the world."

"HIS truth? His own twisted brand of it!" That sorry story is only fit for a dime store rag. Oh yes, I get that disgusting worm. He is all important; no one matters except him. He never takes responsibility, or admits his fuck-ups; everyone has used and abused him. That Creep never had it so bad. He's never slept on the streets or begged for food;" Elizabeth spits out, incensed.

"Relax. I wasn't agreeing with him or anything. Nor, would I ever justify what he did. It's just that sometimes when some people go through bad experiences, they adopt a sick attitude towards others and the world. This sick attitude becomes part of their personality."

"Yeah, whatever. He's never going to tell me or anyone else, anything about Tabitha. Except maybe a few lies, to push it all in our faces."

"How did he react toward you?"

"At first, he either wanted me to fawn over him or to manipulate me. Then, he expected me to cower before him. The coward actually thought he could man-handle me. That's not likely!

"Yeah, I hear you got him good," Klay said, grinning.

"I wish I had got a better shot at him."

"I know what you mean." Klay silently reflected that Elizabeth sometimes lost sight of the bigger picture. But she sure had some raw, pragmatic views that were dead on, accurate.

David had another early delivery scheduled; his alarm went off a couple of hours before normal. Ally couldn't get back to sleep. She went into the living room to watch the morning news. She drifted off to sleep again in the middle of the broadcast.

Once more, Ally was back in Eric's head within her vision. He was driving down a dirt road in the dead of night. As he switched on the interior light, Eric glances through the rear-view mirror at a young girl. The child isn't gagged, nor are her hands or feet bound. But, she is sitting frozen in a stiff fashion, her vacant eyes staring ahead into space. Not even weeping, the girl failed to utter a single sound.

Through his reflection in the mirror, Ally saw Eric's eyes blink, and his head jerked away as if in surprise. He now looks over his shoulder to stare at the child before him.

"What are you a retard or something?" Eric demanded harshly. The child did not respond, no flinch or movement of any kind. She never even looked in his direction. It was as if she hadn't heard him. Her lack of reaction was disconcerting to Eric; he started pounding his fist against the steering wheel. "This is no good, no good at all!"

Ally could see a small travel trailer pulled off the side of the road up ahead through the beam of the headlights. This isolated trailer appeared foreboding in the diminutive light. Smudged, blackened lines etched down the exterior walls; Ally figured that a fire must have damaged the trailer. As she expected, Eric pulled off the road around the rear side of this miserable-looking camper.

Eric jumped out of his Jeep Cherokee with flashlight in hand, shutting the driver side door. He rapidly moved to the rear passenger side door to retrieve the small child. He hauled the girl up under his left arm, pushing the door closed with his right shoulder. With the child in tow, he made his way inside the trailer and turned on a battery operated lamp. Then, he dumped her onto the floor.

Eric pulled out his knife, displaying it in front of the child, as he stared at the girl huddled on the floor. The child failed to register a reaction; her expression remained stagnant. He pressed the knife against the soft skin of the child's face causing a small cut to bleed. Still, she remained expressionless, staring blankly ahead. Nor did the poor babe ever utter a cry or draw away from him. Eric drew back, putting the knife back in his scabbard. He started restlessly pacing back and forth, rubbing his jawline.

Impulsively, Eric grabbed a camera from the counter. He propped up the little girl against the wall; standing up, he flashed a photo of the child. Suddenly, intermittent spots of filtered light glared through the trailer window. Swiftly, Eric returned the camera to the counter. He took out a roll of duct tape from the pocket of his jacket. Hastily, he bound the arms and legs of his young victim, tearing the tape with his teeth. He finished by covering her mouth with a piece of tape. "Just in case," he muttered. Then, he threw a jacket on top of the bound girl. Looking out the window, he tried to gage who was coming up the deserted road.

Light streamed through the windows of the trailer and Ally heard a vehicle stop, right outside on the roadway. Eric stood in rigid stillness as he heard a knock on the door. He was slowly propelled forward to respond to the summons. He opened the door to find two uniformed officers.

"Ummm...What's going on? How can I help you?" Eric asked with mimicked concern, trying to disguise his escalating panic. Ally could see him agitatedly clenching and unclenching his fist behind the trailer door, beyond the scrutiny of the officers.

"Have you been camping here for long?" The officer inquired.

"No, I came up here yesterday for a little R&R." Eric responded. The officer seemed uncomfortable with Eric's presence at this particular site. Or was he, the officer, picking up on Eric's apprehension?

"This isn't a regular campground; there's no set-up accommodations. Why did you choose to camp here?"

"The old Animas mine working are over there," Eric said, pointing his thumb behind him. "I've got a metal detector; I wanted to try my luck in the tailings piles and down at the creek."

"Is this trailer registered?"

"Actually...no sir," Eric said sheepishly. "My cousin has it registered as a non-operational vehicle. A little over a year ago, I bought the trailer from this cousin for next to nothing. Because you see, this trailer got severely damaged in a fire. I've been slowly fixing it up...replaced all the wire and hoses. This trip was my test run to make sure everything was in running order before I transferred the registration."

"I could give you a ticket, but I'll let you off with a warning. You'd better get it registered before you take it out again," the officer replied.

"Thank you, I appreciate it."

"Have you seen anyone else around here?" The officer questioned, looking around the area.

"No. Are you looking for someone?" Eric asked innocently.

"Yes, we're looking for a heavy set woman in her late 30's; early 40's. She is traveling with a young female child, perhaps six years old."

"No, I haven't seen them around here. Do you have a card? I'll give you a call if I see anyone matching that description."

"Just call 911 and report it, if you see them. We'd appreciate your cooperation." The officers headed back to their parked vehicle, unaware that the child, they were looking for, was less than ten feet away.

"That guy sure was acting cagey!" the first officer said. He had waited until they were back in their vehicle before engaging in conversation.

"I picked up on his apprehension too. At first, I thought the guy might have some weed in the trailer or something. But, he didn't look stoned nor could I smell any pot. ...I think he freaked out because the trailer wasn't registered. He probably thought that we would impound it," replied the second officer.

"Yeah, that was my take too;" the first officer said as he put the police car into drive. Eric watched the police car driveaway before slamming the trailer door shut.

"Oh fuck, oh fuck, oh fucking damn!" Eric bellowed as he paced frantically, running his fingers roughly through his hair.

"What the fuck am I going to do? She can't stay here!" Eric continued ranting maniacally to himself. "I can't kill her anywhere near this place. They saw me here! I might be associated with this location or her disappearance. It was so fucking stupid to park this trailer at my encampment. Is this place compromised? Not if I move her out of the area."

"It's dangerous to move her because all the pigs are looking for her. They believe her fucking mother has her. But, those dicks might remember that I was camping out in the area. If that sleazebag mother gets caught, she will tell the dicks that the brat was taken from her. I doubt the pigs would believe her, but they will canvas all the wilderness areas around here. There will be search parties scouring the area. I won't ever be able to come here again." Eric continued hysterically talking to himself, thinking out loud.

"Wait, yes, that's it. In the last two months, there were those two wildfires in Oregon. The fires were out in the national forest, just past the California border. Yes. If a dead kid is found in that region, the authorities will assume the sprog, along with the family, were camping and became casualties of the inferno. Interstate-5 has much more traffic; I won't attract any attention driving down the freeway."

Eric opened the trailer door, surveying the area for any activity. Returning, he grabbed a plaid throw blanket from the chair and rolled the child in it. He dumped the girl on the rear passenger floor with his coat on top of the small pile. Quickly, he started back down the dirt road making his way to the interstate.

"Oh dear God! Tabitha, oh poor Tabitha." Ally moaned as she awoke, rubbing her hands over her eyes to eradicate the images. She could still hear Eric's endless rants in her head. Her sense of doom was palpable, seeming to fill the room. She stood up on quaking legs, trying to relieve the sharp constriction in her chest. Ally held a hand to her throat as she swallowed several times; but, the hard knot there wouldn't dissipate. "I've got to call, Neil," she mumbled, quivering in her shaken state. He'll have to check all the Jane Doe records for young children in southwestern Oregon. But, what if no one ever found Tabitha's body in the forest? Ally questioned dismally.

Would it be fair to pass this information on to Elizabeth, without any concrete proof to back it up? The poor girl is already fed up, and frustrated with all the uncertainties regarding her sister. Then, even if Ally did tell Elizabeth about this vision, and what happened to Tabitha; she knew Elizabeth would never believe her.

Neil still hadn't heard back from George Virtue from *"Mystery Source,"* regarding his request for a supplementary segment on the Morrison matter. He didn't want to be too demanding, but a follow-up telephone call wouldn't hurt.

Neil dialed George's cell phone number, and he promptly answered.

"Hello George, this is Sheriff Neil Bryant. Remember, you produced that segment for *"Mystery Source"* regarding the serial killer, Eric Morrison, from Calaveras County and the possibility of an additional 'unknown' victim?"

"Yes, I remember that piece." George responded.

"Well, there has been an interesting development in this case. Before our department contacted your program about filming that last segment, our men located Morrison's abandoned trailer. In it, there were photos of our known victims before and after their deaths. But, there was one photo of an unidentified child, and she was alive in the photo. We never found any evidence of her death. I couldn't find a missing child case to correlate with the photo. That is the reason our department reached out to your program in the first place. We were hoping to identify this child and find out her status."

"Okay, what's the new development?" he asked with interest.

"A young woman, Elizabeth Lenard, showed up in hopes of finding her missing sister. The little girl was placed in legal guardianship with her aunt. The aunt was mentally unstable and disappeared with the child. In 1992, the child was taken into state custody; later, the aunt kidnaped the child from our county. There have been no sightings of Tabitha since that time. A few years ago, the aunt was picked up; she was living on the streets. She has been institutionalized. This woman cannot give an accurate account of the little girl's whereabouts. It's highly likely that this child is dead, but we simply don't know. I've had an age-enhanced photo produced of Tabitha. We'd like to do a segment regarding Tabitha to see if any additional information materializes."

"It sounds like an interesting story for our program, but we have all our scheduled episodes for this season. Tell you what: I can meet with you and this young lady at my office on August 26, at 10 am to discuss this matter. We can set up a segment to air, next season in September."

"Thank you, I'll contact Ms. Lenard and make the arrangements. I appreciate the meeting." Neil concluded the call.

He called Elizabeth Lenard and left a message on the voice mail giving the date, time, and location of the meeting. He asked her to call to confirm.

Neil was working on some paperwork, when Ally called.

"Hi Neil." Ally didn't wait for Neil to respond. "I've had another vision. It's so horrible! Oh Neil, Eric did kill Tabitha!"

"Ally, slow down and tell me what happened;" Neil instructed her gently.

Ally took a deep breath, and slowly exhaled. Then, she outlined what had happened in her vision.

"What you've told me about the circumstances, makes logical sense; and coincides with the series of events. Sadly, the prognosis for Tabitha doesn't appear promising; I'm certain that Morrison killed her. But remember Ally, we still don't have a body or any tangible proof of her death. We have to carry on as if she's only missing until we find out differently."

"Yes, I know," Ally responded dismally.

"I will check all the relevant death investigation reports in that part of Oregon. Please Ally, don't say anything to Elizabeth or anybody else until we've got 'this matter' all checked out and verified."

"Neil, if Eric dumped her body in the forest, it's possible that her remains were never recovered."

"I know; I hope that's not the case."

"I know what you mean. Elizabeth needs concrete answers."

"I'll let you know what I find." Then Neil said gruffly, "I'm sorry, Ally. You shouldn't have had to witness that nasty scene."

"I'll talk to you later, Neil;," Ally said emotive angst.

Eric set restively on his cot, formulating his escape plan. Getting into the hospital wing, would be a piece of cake. A little over three years ago, he'd received a beat down by one of the prison thugs. He remembered the stupid fuck pounding away on him, yelling, "You tree-jumping Nonce!" That was the equivalent of calling him a child rapist. When Eric was down on the ground, the prick kept kicking him in the head.

Eric had received a traumatic brain injury and since that time, he had the occasional, seizure. He had milked the incident for all it was worth; he could now easily fake a seizure with no effort at all. Each time he seized, he was placed in the hospital wing for several days. He often used this tactic of faking a seizure to evade tricky situations or ward off pending trouble. Eric sneered, it had also got him a constant supply of Clonazepam; he'd used the pills as pay off with the other prisoners for certain favors.

Al owed him a favor! His former cell mate enjoyed the eurphoric high that he got from the Clonazepam in which, Eric had steadily supplied. Al owed him back payments for all the pills, when he was released on parole a few weeks ago. But, his buddy made good on the debt. Eric kissed the fake prison id card that Al had made for him. Just what Eric needed; a man on the outside! For Al, had also managed to get the ID to Cody's bitch, who snuck it into the prison during their conjugal visit. That favor had wiped clean Cody's marker for the Clonazepam too.

In the hospital wing, the early morning shift change took place at 4 am. It was chaotic; supervision was loose. Luckily, many of the staffers over there were new. These newbies wouldn't recognize him. It would be easy to overpower and choke out the lone nurse on duty. With her keys, he would obtain some hospital scrubs. Also, he'd grab some meds and equipment just in case, he ran into another guard who wasn't fooled by the scrubs and this ID card. He was tapping the card against his leg when he heard the guard coming down the corridor. He stuck the card in the top of his sock and pulled down his pant leg. Quickly, he grabbed a magazine, reclining on the cot, and pretended to be reading as the guard pasted by his cell.

Her head was still throbbing; Ally hadn't been able to shed this headache all day. It was a tension headache, brought on by that despicable vision this morning. She took some ibuprofen and went to bed early. Then, the dream began:

Ally was walking down a dirt road under a wide yawn of an expansive, blue-blend sky. Delicate, wispy clouds leisurely stretched out and feathered across this molten, blue backdrop, while hovering black clouds shadowed the setting sun. To her right, brackish mountains were infused in gold, brown, and molten green, springing forth from a field of golden grasses. Ahead, the remaining sunlight glistened off a distant range of mountians, casting the hillside in a spectrum of color. Each mountain emitted an enticing glow; red, a band of pink, and deep purple hues were spectacularly vibrant.

She took a deep breath, absorbing the clean, fresh air as she continued her solitary crossing. All was quiet, except for the soft sounds her feet made as they unsettled the rough ground below. As minutes elapsed, Ally became aware of another presence, accompanying her on this journey. Ally couldn't delineate any shape or form, but intuitively, she knew that her unseen companion was a young child. They traveled for some time in silence.

As they approached a nearby meadow, Ally could hear some archaic melody in the background. She looked up to see a goat with a soft snowy fleece. The lone animal ignored their presence as it continued to graze peacefully on the grasses. Her small companion stopped abruptly; uncertainly, Ally followed suit.

"The goat represents the Greek god, Pan;" her invisible companion narrated. Suddenly, a mirage of shadowy peasants appeared; they formed a semi-circle around the goat. This crowd of translucent peasants applauded and cheered the beast; they adoringly placed a laurel crown upon its head.

"Mischievous Pan was the God of flocks, fertility, and nature. Herein, he brought caprice and folly to the land," her youthful specter explained. The peasants laughed, danced and rejoiced in front of the goat; behind the group laid baskets, filled with produce. The unmindful goat continued to graze.

"But when times were bad...It was all Pan's fault! The goat must be responsible for the bad luck. The peasants would beat Pan, the goat, using shrub-like branches 'squills.' They blamed him for all the ills of society, and for their personal misfortunes." The translucent peasants stealthily encircled the goat; beating him nearly to death. The bleating goat was covered in bloody scratches and cuts.

"This beating was supposed to restore social order and good fortunes. In other words, society used Pan as their 'scapegoat.' But, the goat was simply an animal. Doing what goats do, just as 'it' was born and raised to be." Ally saw the goat along with the peasants evaporate, leaving the meadow vacant.

"But, if the soul of this animal became aware that it was precious and held in high esteem, that it was indeed valuable, what would the goat have become? The deity; it was purported to be? As a kid, the goat should have been primed as to his true stature, his higher purpose." Her companion said in conclusion. A glowing laurel crown appeared, like a halo, in the spot where the goat had stood.

"I'm here to deliver a message," her companion transmitted. "To help you to understand... You need to restore order, wholeness, by helping 'him' to achieve his redemption. I'll guide you and show you the way." Then, her companion was gone. Ally was left standing alone in the secluded meadow. She looked up at the bright nimbus of the remaining sunlight, which reflected sharply from the brown glazed hillside.

What a dream! Ally opened her eyes, running her hands through her hair as she stared at the ceiling above. She tried to piece together the elements of this vision. If this information was imparted to her, it had to be somehow relevant. Her unseen companion must have been alluding to Eric in the metaphor. But, who was this child?

An angel? Ally couldn't detect any visual outline to this being, yet she knew that her companion had been a child. Could it be Bree? Bree had crossed over to the spiritual realm; maybe that is why Ally couldn't discern any clear form. In the early visions, her young friend -Bree had always tried to bring forth information about Eric. Or, was this vision associated with Tabitha in any way? Ally wondered what the locale in the vision revealed. Could Tabitha's remains be in that pasture? Could this young soul, possibly be the spirit of Tabitha trying to communicate with her?

CHAPTER 7

"I can't sit by and wait to meet with the '*Mystery Source*' people. Or hang around, waiting for the show to air. That's over a month away; I've got to keep busy!" Elizabeth interjected as she sat with Klay at the coffee shop.

"Get some perspective, Elizabeth. You've done all that you can do. You need to be patient and let some of your efforts take hold;" Klay rejoined.

"The Sullivan Woman; she doesn't miss a trick. Somehow, she got a peek into that creep -Morrison's playbook. I have to find out how that Sullivan woman found him out. She must have hacked into his computer or found a notebook. What else could it be?"

"Excuse me, you have her take;" Klay countered.

"You mean the ruse she used. If I'm going to find Tabitha, I need to know the truth. Perhaps, I can guilt her into telling me. Or if I catch her off guard, maybe she'll let something slip."

"What if she sticks to her story? Repeats that psychic business; then, what are you going to do?" Klay contemplated; Elizabeth was going to get herself into trouble.

"Then, maybe, I'll have to be the vision in front of her and the voice in her head. ...Until, I find out her secret," Elizabeth mocked.

"If you're not careful, you're going to get yourself into hot water," Klay cautioned. "Have you given Marion your final answer about staying in her house until school starts?"

"No; but, she'll be back home tomorrow."

"If you need help with the answer, phone a friend." Klay pulled out a cell phone with a gift bow, taped onto it. "You need to be available; whenever there is a break in Tabitha's case." Klay handed the phone to her.

"Thanks, Klay, you didn't need to do this," Elizabeth said holding up the phone.

"I know, but I wanted to. And if you're asking me, I want you to stay."

"So I will until I can move into a dorm room."

"You could attend classes at Acacia College this fall. You're already registered there, you know," Klay told her.

"Yes, I am;" she smiled up at him.

Eric worked out vigorously in the weight room as he continued to devise his escape plan. After he retrieved the duty nurse's keys, he would place her in the hospital bed with the linens pulled up over her face. Next, he needed to rig the cameras. He strongly suspected that the security system was a Pyramid model. He was literally betting his ass on it!

He knew about this manufacturer and could utilize the operational functions to circumvent the system. It would be easy to 'blind' the video feed of the camera, monitoring the hospital room, with his LED pen light. Then, he would momentarily interupt the power supply of the system and that of the battery back up, which would cause the system to refresh itself. It should buy him approximately ten minutes.

Eric moved to the treadmills. After he was outside the prison gates, he would make a run for the bus station that was five miles from prison lot. Eric increased his speed on the trendmill as he conceptualizing his escape. He won't be seen if he gets to the station before five in the morning.

Eric looked up at the clock; he had to finish up his workout before the bell rang to go to the mess hall. His plan would have to be placed on hold until later, when he had time to flesh out the details. He started his cool down and treated himself to one of his favorite fantasies. In this fantasy, Eric visualized sticking a knife in the Bitch-Ally's gut. Then, he would slit the throat of the maggot as the Bitch bled out. Eric snickered, as he imagined the helpless horror in her face as the inevitable happened.

Ally drove up into her driveway, when she noticed an older vehicle pulling in behind her. Glancing through the rear-view mirror, Ally recognized the young woman in the driver's seat. It was Elizabeth. Ally got out of her car as Elizabeth walked towards her. Ally hoped this conversation wouldn't take long because Breanna was still in her toddler seat in the back seat of the car.

"You know I don't believe in all the psychic shit you were feeding me. But, you had an inside line on that Morrison creep. I need to know how you got your information. It could be important!" Elizabeth challenged.

"I'm sorry; I've got nothing more to tell you about the investigation." Ally looked uncomfortable and eager to escape.

"I don't give a damn what you told the cops or anybody else. I won't give you away. I just want to find out how you came across the goods on Morrison. Following this trail, might lead me to Tabitha." Elizabeth coaxed.

"I've nothing solid to add to the investigation." Ally swallowed hard, trying to cover up her slip; avoiding eye contact with Elizabeth. She didn't want the girl to read anything in her expression.

"But, you have more information?" Elizabeth stared intently at Ally. "You know something that you're not telling me! I see it in your face." Elizabeth demanded as Ally tried to turn away. Then, Elizabeth stepped in front of Ally, blocking her path.

"I've had some more visions but I've got no solid leads on your sister," Ally said in a rushed voice.

"You said that you didn't get visions anymore. Now, you do again. How fucking convenient! Tell me what you know about Tabitha."

"I'm sorry I can't," Ally agonized.

"You mean you won't! It's my sister! What kind of twisted bitch are you?" Elizabeth yelled.

"Please move out of my way! My daughter is upset," Breanna was crying in the backseat; Ally attempted to push Elizabeth aside in order to reach her daughter. David witnessed with alarm the confrontation between Ally and this young woman as he drove up and parked, along the front of the house. What in the world is going on? Breanna is crying for God's sake! Ally should know better, David thought crossly. His baby shouldn't be exposed to this heated confrontation.

"Not until you tell me about Tabitha," Elizabeth shouted.

"I don't know who you are or what you're doing here. But, you'd better get off my property before I call the police." David barked as he headed to Ally's car to get Breanna out of her car seat.

"Ally, come inside the house now, before this argument escalates any further." He headed towards the front door of the house, comforting a crying Breanna in his arms.

"I'll let you know when I have any viable information," Ally said, then followed David inside.

"I'm coming back again. Do you hear me!" Elizabeth yelled as Ally shut the door.

"What the hell was that all about?" David abruptly demanded, turning towards Ally after she shut the front door. He took a deep breath, trying to curb his annoyance.

"That young woman is Elizabeth. She's the sister of the
114

missing girl."

"So...what's up? Why is she mad at you?" David coolly inquired as he sat Breanna down on the couch, patted the top of her head, and looked back towards Ally.

"She thinks I have additional information about her sister;" Ally said sheepishly, diverting her gaze towards the door.

"Do you?" David inquired, giving her a funny look.

"YES!" Ally said in a whine, "Her sister is dead, but I don't have any concrete proof to support the claim."

"Oh God, no, not again!" David said beseechingly.

"Yes," Ally said, letting out a deep breath with heavy resignation. "I've got to call Neil and see if he has any more information about Tabitha." David looked skyward, running his hands down over his eyes in frustration.

Ally went over to phone Neil. After the familiar greetings, she cut to the chase.

"Neil, I just had an unpleasant encounter with Elizabeth. ...She wanted to 'really know' how I got the 'goods' on Eric. I told her that I had no additional information to offer. But, I've got no poker face; she knows something is up. She confronted me about keeping secrets about Tabitha. I admitted to having new visions, but I explained that nothing tangible had surfaced. I gave her the brush off, but I'm sure she's going to have 'a go' at me again. Have you found out any more about her sister?"

"Ally, there were two wildfires in Oregon, the summer before Tabitha went missing. The Rogue River fire in June of 1992 and the East Evan Creek fire in August of 1992, which matches our timeline. Morrison could have taken Tabitha and dumped her body there in September of that year. But, I've found no death investigations or inquiries in southwestern Oregon, which correlate with Tabitha's data since that time. I'm sorry that I'm no closer to having any definite answers."

"Thank you, Neil, for the update. I'll try to avoid any further confrontations with Elizabeth," Ally finished the call.

"That woman knows something, and she's not saying it! But, I know she was about to crack; when the husband showed up and threatened to call the cops on me." Elizabeth told Klay when she met up with him, later that evening.

"Okay Elizabeth! You know what they say about attracting more bees with honey. It won't do you any good to get a restraining order placed against you."

"But Klay, it's Tabitha! I've got to find out what that Sullivan woman knows," Elizabeth fumed.

"I'll give Dad a call; maybe he can get some answers from Sullivan." Klay went inside Marion's house to call. Klay returned a short time later.

"Dad knows something. He has already spoken to Alyssa Sullivan about a possible lead. So, he's got this new lead; as yet, it hasn't panned out. He told me that he'd call you, when he was sure 'this lead is credible and not beforehand.'"

"How fucking great is that?" Elizabeth said in exacerbation.

"He also wanted me to tell you, to stay out of it, and to lay off Ally. Ally is passing any information she receives to him so it can be verified, and then dutifully investigated."

"No way! I'm not going to just sit here doing nothing while they play their little game."

"Elizabeth, I know you're upset. But, I do believe everyone is taking Tabitha's disappearance seriously. I hope you can put some trust in that fact."

"Yes, whatever you say;" Elizabeth quipped. She felt a little bit peevish; because she did realize that after all, Klay was only trying to help.

Later that night, Ally laid awake in bed for a long time; the confrontation with Elizabeth reverberated in her mind. "I don't have anything definitive to offer the poor girl. With the information from my vision, Elizabeth wouldn't be any better off than she is now. In fact, it might be far worse for her." Ally, however, wasn't convinced that she was doing the right thing. If Tabitha's remains hadn't been located in that Oregon wilderness since 1992, it was highly unlikely that any traces of the child would be found anytime soon, if ever. Elizabeth's futile and unrelenting search would continue, when Ally knew the dismal truth. There was no winning solution to this dilemma. Finally, Ally fell asleep and started dreaming.

Ally was under an ample sky; the white of the horizon gradually intensified to a deep, drowsy blue. In each direction, a range of blackened mountains stood at differing depths and proximity; and thus, gave this vibrant scenery a three-dimensional quality. The outline of these coarse ranges formed jagged borders with crisp and clean lines, bringing a sharp finale to the sprawling heavens. The pictureque setting appeared overly authentic; as if it were concocted to look excessively genuine by an artist's skillful hand.

Centered ahead in the distance, stood a snow-capped mountain peak shrouded in the mass of a single cloud under the vast expanse of blue hues. The cloaked summit seemingly emanated an aura of mystery; forecasting that profound answers lay at its foundation. Suddenly, Ally was being propelled forward, toward this very spot.

At the base of this mountainous peak, with the low lying cloud, there was a cave emitting a phantom mist. "And beyond..." like she used to say to her good friend, Jennie. Ally mused that any source of knowledge laid far past the footing of this peak, within the endless 'eternal' depths of this cavern. She no longer attempted to make logical sense of this odd vision when she again felt the presence of her 'angel' messenger.

Her unseen companion had returned. And now, Ally was

certain that this unseen entity wasn't Bree; for 'it' didn't have the same feel. Ally ventured that this youthful spirit was older than Bree. And, this presence had a different expressive style, failing to engage Ally personally in the exchange of conversation.

The young messenger calls out, "Each living entity has a core of energy or life force; a soul, as well as a spirit. The spirit has a distinctive essence which is reflective of that life form. You see the raven overhead. It is said that its spirit brings forth his own special magic of illumination, a bringer of light to help people." The vanishing bird left a half circle trail of light that brighten the cave entrance in its wake. The radiance of this light illuminated the provincial people below; in the center, a young boy stood in proximity to the mouth of the cave.

A beautiful white leopard emerged through the mist from the interior of the cave. The messenger says, "The spirit of the snow leopard imbibes the purity of the blood, leaving the weakness of the flesh behind." The leopard advanced on a little boy; snarling, ready to attack. The group of gawkers stood by, watching the pending attack.

The messenger said quietly, "each person is watching, waiting for the others to intervene. Meanwhile, the child is destroyed." The leopard swoops in on the boy. He crumbles into a scrunched heap, trying to protect himself.

"The purity of the youth is gone, leaving the desecrated, hollow casing in its stead." The flaccid youth appeared dead. The big cat turned away from the child; steadfastly, eyeing the town folk. The weakened boy urgently crept away and made haste towards the mouth of the cave for safety.

Suddenly, a puma sprang out through the mist, past the leopard and towards the crowd of townsmen. Another vicious animal was on the attack! The beast glared with wild, stricken eyes at each of the frantic villagers, in turn, before lashing out and wounding several people in the crowd. The mountain lion bit down on one of the natives, wounding a horrified woman.

"Whereas, the puma spirit devours the flesh, absorbing the weaknesses; therein, leaving behind the blood, regardless of the purity," the narrator recounted. The mirage of villagers along with the animals dissolved; but, the cave entrance with that peculiar mist remained.

The presence was dissipating as the voice trailed off towards the cave entry. "The poor boy is such a wretched soul; sorely missing his enlightened spirit! He could be lost forever in darkness without an intact soul. But, he can be made whole once again; the destitute soul can be reunited with the elusive spirit. It's the only way, the situation can be made right and hence, advancement made on his eternal path. ...You, Ally, must save yourself and thus reassert life."

"Oh God!" Ally roughly rubbed her eyes as she awoke. Another parable? What did these fables and allegories mean? And what does this vision have to do with me? It was similar to a foreign language that she couldn't fully grasp. She simply didn't speak: metaphor! How was she supposed to utilize this information in such a way that it would yield cogent results? Should she tell Neil about these visions? The imagery was far too abstract. These dreams left Ally feeling like she was irrational or crazy again; like it had been in the very beginning, when she first encountered Bree.

"How did the meeting go, dear?" Marion inquisitively asked as Elizabeth entered the house.

Marion is so concerned! Elizabeth could see it in her eyes. She had met this plump, older woman with the short, dark hair a little over a week ago. Surprisingly, she felt instantly at ease with the lady and had readily opened up to Marion about Tabitha.

"Good News. The producers of 'Mystery Source,' want to film the segment about Tabitha, next week, and have it air the first week in September."

"That's wonderful for you, Elizabeth! That way, you won't be preoccupied with the show, at the same time that you're starting your classes. You have enough on your plate as it is."

"I got lucky, I guess. Some new information came forth about another story that had been scheduled to air on the program. Mr. Virtue wanted to delay this segment until he had all the new developments. So, he wanted to substitute this other segment with the one about my sister." Earlier this week, Elizabeth received a call from the secretary from 'Mystery Source,' asking to move up their appointment date to today.

"I sure hope this program can give us some answers soon."

"I need to call Klay. I promised him that I'd give him an update as soon as I got out of the meeting," Elizabeth responded as she pulled out her cell phone.

Eric rigidly rocked to and fro as he sat on the bunk, constructing the final details of his escape plan. He despised the idea of relying on others in his plan. But, he didn't see any way around it.

His pal, Sam was a loner, somewhat of a recluse. But, the old man had taken a shine to him when they met over ten years ago. Eric had been metal detecting at the river, near Sam's rustic cabin when they struck up an unlikely friendship. Often, Eric would stop and offer Sam a cup of coffee from his thermos when he was in the vicinity of his place.

His aged pal never asked any questions; never wanted to know anything. Eric paid old Sam, twenty bucks a month to park the jeep on his property. Eric would call Sam and offer him a hundred dollars to bring his jeep to the bus station. Without a doubt, he knew Sam would do this favor for him with no questions asked. After Eric dropped Sam off at his place, he would stop at the wreckage yard and nab a different set of license plates for the jeep.

The rocking became vehement. He'd collect the emergency cash that he had stashed away before he contacted former cell-mate Al, again. He would use his remaining pills and any other drugs he obtained from the medicine cabinet in the hospital, to pay off Al for a fake driver's license. Yes, he'd have all the supplies, he needed to alter his appearance for the ID when he met up with his old buddy, Al.

Yes, his plan was falling into place; his movements became increasingly erratic. When would he execute the plan? Eric slammed his fist repeatedly into his lap; think, think, think.....Labor Day weekend! Security always seemed more lax around holiday weekends; personnel taking time off. Yes, that was it!

Just you wait, Bitch! An image of the Sullivan's dismembered body formed in his mind. In a flash, a vision of his mother eclipsed that of the Bitch. Eric grabbed his hair tightly on each side of his head, his body curled into itself; until he laid motionless in a fetal position. His wild, stricken eyes stared intensely ahead at the wall of his cell.

Elizabeth parked outside the Sullivan woman's cul-de-sac and waited. Her stake-out lasted about an hour and a half, but finally the woman drove past her car. She followed the woman to a daycare center and watched as she took the toddler inside. Roughly ten minutes later, Sullivan returned to her car and pulled away.

Elizabeth followed the woman to a county building, quickly parking her car to catch up with Sullivan. She hurried into the building looking for the Sullivan woman through the milling people. Finally, she caught sight of Alyssa Sullivan and made her way towards her. But, that Bitch must have spotted her for she conveniently disappeared into one of the offices.

Elizabeth headed back to her car to wait for Sullivan in the parking lot. But, the woman didn't appear. Elizabeth waited as long as she could, but she had an appointment with the film crew for 'Mystery Source.' Oh well, that Bitch of a woman couldn't evade her forever. Elizabeth was going to get some answers!

Ally arrived home with another tension headache. Her casework at the Family Preservation Coalition was often frustrating. She had been unsuccessful in her attempt to persuade a teenage mother, Taylor, to re-enroll in night school. Boy, that girl was stubborn; none of her arguments have even dented the girl's resolve. And then, there was Elizabeth Lenard! She caught sight of the young woman tailing her and barely escaped the encounter.

Ally felt guilty for avoiding the girl. But, she was fearful that she would give something away if she spoke directly with Elizabeth. Indecisive, Ally was still unclear on whether or not she was being fair to Elizabeth by keeping her vision about Tabitha secret. She hoped that Neil would uncover some evidence in Tabitha's case soon.

Ally went inside and laid down. Amazingly, she fell asleep. Shortly, she was dreaming another vision:

Ally stood next to her unseen companion under a star-filled sky. Only a small, slip of an incandescent, crescent moon was visible overhead. Campfire flames flickered merrily away in a forest clearing, twenty feet away enfolded by a boundary of tall trees. A strange flute-like tune sounded next to her in the night. Her companion played the haunting melody and then abruptly stopped.

The unseen youth began to narrate, "The shepard's pipe is used to invoke the animal spirits or the ancient ones." A flute hovers out mid-air into the clearing; again, playing the haunting tune. "We ask the ancient ones for wisdom and guidance in our times of need." A mirage of translucent animals along with a Native American tribe stood just outside the perimeter of the campfire.

A shirtless man, in a bull-horned headdress, stood adjacent to the campfire. He carried something strung out between his hands. Then he began a ritualized dance, like an ancient Native American. As he passed in front of the campfire light, Ally let out a gasp, "Eric!"

Yes! Eric was dancing in front of the fire with a rattlesnake in tow!

"In Greek mythology, the Minotaur had the head of a bull and the body of a man. He devours youth and destroys the innocent," the youth narrated. "But as you see, the archetype of the human beast lives on in many cultures and survives throughout the ages."

"Native Americans believed that poisonous snakes stimulate primal energies which can cure rather than kill." The narrator informed as if pointing out various elements in the scene.

The snake bites Eric. As Eric starts to slump forward, the aura of her unseen companion moves towards him. Her narrator gradually manifests into a discernable form of a youthful boy. The spirit boy steps in front of the adult –Eric. The phantom boy infiltrated and morphed into Eric.

The boy's voice trails off, "The spirit is reunited with the soul; the spiritualized soul is restored to wholeness once again. The beast man receives redemption. Renewal occurs, and spiritual soul continues onward……"

"Oh my dear, God!" Ally tried to wrap her mind around the images. Her unseen companion was Eric, and his spirit was trying to communicate with her. Did that mean that Eric was dead? Ally needed to call Neil! It was going to be hard to wait until morning. She had to find out Eric's status.

"Neil," Ally said wildly as soon as he answered the phone. "I need you to find out if something has happened to Eric Morrison."

"Ally, what's going on? You seem overwrought," Neil said with concern.

"Neil, I've been receiving some strange and abstract visions. I haven't been able to discern how these visions relate to the investigation into Tabitha's disappearance. Last night, I had a vision of Eric's death."

"I see, I'll call the prison; and make some inquiries about Morrison. I'll give you a call back in about fifteen minutes." Ally waited next to the phone until Neil called back.

"Ally. ...Eric Morrison is still alive. But, he was sent to the medical ward last night. He is being treated for a seizure disorder."

"Alright," Ally was perplexed. "I know these visions must have some meaning or significance. But, what that meaning is, beats the heck out of me."

"I'll talk to you later. I've got to finish up my work with the film crew for '*Mystery Source*.' The producers play to air the segment on Tabitha at the end of next week," Neil concluded.

CHAPTER 8

Elizabeth wasn't at a dead end! There was still some action to be taken in her sister's case. As yet, Elizabeth still hadn't challenged that Sullivan woman and wheedled the information about Tabitha from her. The bitch was surely holding back this info as her 'ace in the hole.' She must be mucked deeply in the mire. Maybe she could face criminal charges; in the way she got the dope on Morrison? Yes, that had to be it.

What was that Sullivan woman's 'take' in this scenario anyway? If the woman had been in it for the money, then why hadn't she cashed in on the 'psychic scam'? In addition, that woman was still in league with the cops. Why? And it wasn't as if the 'death threat' that the Creep had asked her to give to that Sullivan woman was personalized in any way like they shared complicity in the crimes. But, Elizabeth knew that she must have overlooked some connection between the two of them.

Elizabeth retrieved the legal brief that Cheryl Weiss had prepared for her, weeks ago. Unsettled, her fingers drummed against the document. Had she overlooked anything else in this report? It wouldn't hurt to review it again for any possible leads.

Elizabeth opened the brief, hoping to uncover any new material. She skimmed through the report before perusing it more carefully. She read the social and educational history on the Creep. Yes, she was right; Elizabeth thought resentfully. Morrison came from money. He'd never had to worry about where he was going to sleep because he'd had a decent home. There was always food on the table at his house.

"Wait a minute here," Elizabeth interjected. What had she just missed? Elizabeth carefully reread the prior section. The Creep's paternal grandmother ...her last name was listed as 'Michael;' his grandmother must have remarried. Why did that surname sound so familiar? Elizabeth had seen that name in another context.

Where had she seen that last name before? Elizabeth quickly flipped through the report looking for the last name of 'Michael'. Ahh huh, there was her answer in the witness statements! Oh my God, that Sullivan woman. Her full name was Alyssa Joan 'Michael' Sullivan; ...her maiden name was 'Michael.'

"It was a family affair! That fucking bitch must be distantly related to the Creep! Someone in the family must have filled her in, on what Morrison was up to. That was her 'in' on this investigation. The Sullivan woman tried to stop the Creep before their relationship was exposed. No wonder, she was so tight lipped. Who could blame her? She didn't want her association with the Creep to be made public. She didn't want to air the family's dirty laundry.

What a beaut! Eric reflected on his recent escape from the prison. He was free and clear of that fucking rat hole! He sat with his knees bent on the asphalt ground, with his back against a cement pillar. As, he listened to the sound of the traffic moving overhead, on the overpass above. Yes; his plan had gone off without a hitch. But, there was one exception.

Eric considered the killing of the nurse to be anticlimactic. He revived the memory of this most recent kill. Eric visualized the nurse's head, locked within the clamp of his half-nelson; his downward gaze was fastened upon the dark-blond hair below. He recreated the feel of tension in his forearm, by tightly clenching his fist. He recalled the feel of the nurse's neck under his arm as he choked the life out of her. Eric reenacted the gesture as he physically formed the motion of a half-nelson. His labored breathing hissed erratically in the still air. The initial wild struggle of the cunt; rapidly gave way to dead weight. Eric let his arm fall, leadenly downward as if releasing this tension with his eyes staring intensely ahead. Then, he placed the dead woman onto the hospital bed and drew the bed linens over her lifeless form, partially covering her face.

"Simply, a waste!" Eric ruminated, shaking his head fervently. Even this rendition of his actions, failed to arouse any excitement at all.   There was no release of his pent-up tension; because, it had happened far too quickly. Ultimately, the woman was dead before she even knew it. He hadn't been able to take any time to slow down, and savor the fear of that nurse. He hadn't had the chance to even stare into the cunt's eyes as he choked her out.

It'll be different with the Sullivan Bitch! Eric planned to take his good ol' sweet time, pace himself nicely. He had waited, anticipated this killing, for far too long. He wouldn't rush it! Forlornly, Eric acknowledged that he wouldn't have the luxury of time to hash out all the details of the pending abduction. He had to grab the Bitch with her pod, as quickly as possible before the pigs caught wind of his trail. No matter, Eric sneered; he would make up for this time inadequacy with the elongated, bloody massacre of the Bitch and that of her spawn.

He knew exactly, where to take his 'prey.' Last week, he'd heard on the news that that Hemsdale project was to be shut down for several weeks. The site would be vacant. Eric knew the general area; it was isolated. But to be sure, he'd take a drive and scope out the area. But he was certain that the project site would afford him the privacy and time, which he needed to fully execute the slaughters while relishing the experience.

Afterward, he planned to leave his calling card. He would place the decapitated head of the pod child at his sister's front door. Dear sweet, Caitlyn would shit a brick when she read the accompanying message; written in blood: "Your spawn is next!" Then onward to the asshole; Sheriff Neil Bryant's house to leave the Bitch's head with the bloody message, "checkmate!" Eric was getting giddy, feeling his body tauten in anticipation. He started rocking rapidly to and fro; eager to begin.

There was no time to dawdle; he'd have to move quickly. Eric jumped up and determinedly moved towards his Jeep. Soon, he'd put his scheme into motion. First, he'd examine the project site and verify its appropriateness. Or, make the necessary accommodations! Then, he would stake out the strip mall, closest to the Bitch's residence. Of course, she would shop close to her own home. He wouldn't fuck up by being stupid enough to be seen near her house.

Elizabeth was restless! She shouldn't be moving into the dorm today. She needed to remain here! Why had she let Klay persuade her into this move so soon anyway? His father, Sheriff Bryant, had probably talked Klay into 'getting her out of the way.' She could've waited another week or two before relocating to the college.

The segment of *'Mystery Source'* would premiere tonight. What if there was any new information on Tabitha? She couldn't respond quickly to the scene or be on top of any new leads from Acacia. Elizabeth also couldn't track down and confront that Sullivan woman as easily from her dorm room.

"Elizabeth, is everything packed up, and in the car? Marion and Jeannie have lunch waiting for us," Klay informed her.

"Give me five minutes; then I'll be ready."

"Okay, I'll let them know," Klay called out, as he made his way towards the kitchen. Elizabeth was also going to miss Marion's company. But, she'd promised to keep in touch with Marion after she moved into the dorms.

Neil obsessed as he scrutinized all the 'Jane Doe' death records for all children roughly Tabitha's age. From 1992 onward, he poured through the cases throughout Oregon and also within Northern California. Again, there were no possible matches on file.

Damn! Neil couldn't even come up with a plausible ploy to activate a massive search for this child. Besides, it wouldn't do any good unless the Oregon authorities could scope in on a likely location. Would the segment in that news program produce any credible leads?

Neil contemplated using the segment from *'Mystery Source'* to facilitate a minor deception but not without a feeling of guilt. After the show had aired, Neil could inform the Oregon authorities that he received a possibly lead on the hotline. An anonymous caller reported seeing a man resembling Eric Morrison with a young girl matching Tabitha's description. The man and child got out of a parked Jeep in the National Forest, just past the Stateline. The caller remembered the encounter from 1992; because the man appeared suspicious. He seemed nervous and the child, fearful. ...It was a small, white lie! Especially since this time, Ally's vision was comprehensive and detailed.

The phone rang, interrupting Neil's thoughts. He moved to pick up the line.

"Hello, Sheriff Neil Bryant speaking."

"Sheriff Bryant, this is Glenn Vanderberg. I'm the warden of Valley Correctional Facility." The man hesitated warily and then continued. "The inmate Eric Morrison, escaped from our prison, earlier this morning. I'm about to issue a special news bulletin regarding this matter."

"How in the Hell did that happen?" Neil demanded, "Morrison was placed in maximum security."

"The inmate was admitted to the medical wing. Nothing usual about this hospitalization because Morrison suffers from an ongoing seizure disorder." The warden continued defensively, "While, under medical supervision, he killed the duty nurse and managed to circumvent the surveillance cameras. We're probing into the possible methods; he employed to get outside the gates."

"I'm grateful for the head's up," Neil said somberly. "I've got to notify several individuals of the pending danger and issue extra patrols in each of their neighborhoods."

"I'll keep you informed of any developments," Vanderberg concluded the call.

Ally arrived with Breanna at the daycare center. It was earlier than usual because Ally had a busy day ahead with several extensive appointments scheduled. In a rush, she grabbed Breanna's lunch box and backpack before opening the rear passenger door to get Breanna out of the car.

As Ally led her daughter into the building, she had a sudden, but very odd feeling. It was as if she were looking at Breanna from a distance. As if, Ally was looking at Breanna for the last time. She would never see her daughter again. Disturbed, Ally fought the urge to cling onto Breanna's hand as her daughter broke away to greet one of her young friends.

"Cut it out, for crying out loud;" Ally chided, unnerved by her current train of thoughts. As in trepidation, Ally watched a carefree Breanna playing with her friend. It was all these strange dreams that were making her so apprehensive. That's all it is! Shaking off the dismay, she reluctantly left the building. With renewed determination, Ally purposefully turned her concentration to upcoming meeting with Madison.

What goals should they focus on today? She mentally outlined the proposed objectives for the week. Hopefully, Madison would be on the same page. Ally reminded herself to verify whether Madison finished her vocational aptitude testing at the junior college. Arriving for her appointment with Madison, Ally turned off her cell phone so they wouldn't be interrupted.

Ally continued from one appointment to the next. At 11:30, Ally stopped to collect her messages. Neil left a message for her to call him. Maybe he found out some information about Tabitha. Well, she didn't have time to speak with him right now. She'd call when she got home and had finished her appointments for the day.

Ally stopped at the dry cleaners; she received a message that her clothing was ready for pick-up. The cleaners were on her way to Breanna's daycare. Hurriedly, she rushed inside, eager to finish her tasks for the day. Ally was anxious to get back home and call Neil.

Arriving at Fordham Hall, Elizabeth and Klay unloaded the car, transferring Elizabeth's belongings to her dorm room. Klay went downstairs to retrieve another load. When Klay returned to the room he appeared strained, worried about something.

"Okay give, what's up?" Elizabeth questioned cautiously.

"Just got a call from Dad. He wanted to let us know that Eric Morrison escaped from prison this morning. He didn't want you or me to hear about his escape on the news."

"Okay, I bet he'll be back behind bars soon enough. If we're lucky, he'll get shot, trying to evade capture. He's of no use to me! The Creep is never going to tell me the truth about Tabitha."

"You're right. Dad says it usually doesn't take very long to recapture escaped fugitives. Also, he wanted to warn you. Dad doesn't believe that Morrison will try to come after you. But, he wants you to be on your guard and avoid being by yourself until he is apprehended."

"That Creep won't take a crack at me. The asshole is too afraid that I'd strike back. I'd tear him apart, and he knows it," Elizabeth said fiercely.

"Like it or not, Morrison is a survivor. I'm sure he'll kill or be killed, rather than face going back to prison. You don't want to place yourself in the middle of that kind of desperation." Klay said gingerly, noting Elizabeth's' inflexible stance.

"Yes. The Creep will throw a huge temper tantrum if things don't go as he plans. But like I told you, he won't come anywhere near me. For this reason, unfortunately, I won't be able to enjoy the show!" Elizabeth spat out.

"Okay, let's get finished up here. That news program starts at seven," Klay said firmly, changing the subject.

Eric surveyed the small strip mall; it consisted of a nail salon, a hardware store, a market, dry cleaners, and a pizzeria along with a few other small shops. He parked his Jeep along the outer parameter of the parking lot, where he could easily view each vehicle as it entered the complex. He continued to keep the entrance under surveillance for many hours.

Eric lost track of the time, as he stared intently at a solitary ingress into the center. Low and behold, the Bitch pulled in and parked in the first vertical stall and hurriedly headed into the dry cleaners.

It was good to have friends in low places! Thanks to Sam and Al, he was already in position to grab her. He smirked as he doused the rag with chloroform that Al had brought to him. He grabbed his tool kit when he exited the Jeep.

He glanced around; there was no one visible in the vicinity of her car. He crouched down in front of her Ford Taurus in the shadow of a tree, which stood amid the island. He watched her approach and unlock the driver's side door. As the Bitch bent forward to hang the clothing in the back seat, he surged towards her, clamping the rag over her nose. Quickly, he opened the rear door, pushing the Bitch's inert form onto the floorboard of the car.

Glancing up, disappointed, Eric noted the empty child seat in front of him. "Oh, fucking great! Her spawn wasn't with her. He'd have to revise the plan. He grabbed her car keys, which had fallen to the ground. He climbed into the driver's seat, started the engine, and put the car into reverse.

Eric pulled into a secluded, vacant lot; a couple of blocks from the shopping center. He bound and gagged the Bitch before he proceeded with the injection. He'd got the sedative along with the syringe, from the medicine cabinet within the prison. Good, now he was ready to head towards Hemsdale.

As Eric pulled back onto the roadway, he heard the Sullivan Bitch's cell phone ring. Yes, the authorities could track those things. He located the phone; opened the window and tossed the phone away. Good riddance!

Neil was apprehensive. Something wasn't right; he still hadn't heard back from Ally, and it was almost three in the afternoon. It could be that she was simply busy and hadn't bothered to check her messages. Neil called her cell phone again; it went straight to voicemail. This time, when he left the message for her to call him immediately; he wasn't concerned about alarming her.

Neil turned on the television set in the stationhouse; in order to hear the special news bulletin. It was the typical alert; he thought as he switched off the TV. Surely, someone, out in the public, would spot Morrison and phone in about the sighting. He also knew that every law enforcement agency and every law enforcement officer was on the watch for Morrison, in this state and nationally. It was just a matter of time until Morrison was recaptured.

C'mon Ally, phone for God's sake! Neil started pacing to and fro. That's it; he was going to call David at the supermarket. Neil only hoped that he wouldn't panic David, 'needlessly.'

"Hello, could I speak with the store manager, David Sullivan?" Neil paused for the response, then said, "No, I don't want to leave a message. This is Sheriff Neil Bryant. Could you page Mr. Sullivan?" Neil waited impatiently, slapping his hand against the desktop.

When David answered, Neil said quickly,"Yes, David. This is Neil. I don't want to upset you, but Eric Morrison escaped from prison this morning. I tried to call your wife and put her on alert. But, Ally hasn't returned my messages. I need to talk to her," Neil finished.

"Oh dear God, no! Not again," David said desperately. "If that son-of-bitch hurts Ally, I'm going to kill the bastard myself!"

"David, I understand your feelings. I'm sure that Ally is fine, probably hasn't picked up her messages. I just want her to be aware of the situation, so we can keep her safe." Neil said unconvincedly, trying to keep the skepticism out of his tone.

"First, I'll call Ally's supervisor, Connie, and find out if Ally clocked out for the day. Next, I'll call the daycare, and find out if Ally has picked up Breanna yet. Then, I'll run by the house and see if she's home," David rattled off his list.

"David, give me the license plate number to Ally's car. I'll issue a 'be on the lookout alert" for her car."

"GMP 329," David offered as Neil wrote down the number.

"Please, call me back later with the update," Neil concluded the call.

It had been several hours since Neil had phoned David. There still had been no word from Ally. Neil had phoned the hospital; Ally hadn't been admitted nor had anyone matching her description. The hotline received one call regarding a possible sighting of Morrison, traveling southbound on Highway 47 near Prospector Hill. Neil studied the regional maps and sent officers to scour several remote locations within that vicinity. Morrison liked the wilderness areas; it was his domain.

Neil listened to dispatch on the police radio. He was analyzing the calls for any possible leads to Morrison or any information that might be linked to Ally. A call came through dispatch from the watchman at the Hemsdale Water Irrigation Project. He reported trespassers on the site. Hemsdale had been in the news lately; Neil cogitated. The project had temporarily been shut down until some environmental issues could be rectified. The Hemsdale Project was exactly the kind of place Morrison would choose as a hideout. It was remote enough, and Morrison was technically savvy. He'd had all those technology trade magazines along with his porno collection when the Sheriff's office had searched his apartment back in '98. Neil was going to follow up on this lead himself; he headed out the door.

Ally tried to zero in and distinguish what she was seeing. But, the image kept fading in and out of focus as the light fell upon and retracted from the immediate area. The pattern was composed of connected circles. A frosted metal mesh? What was that straight line above the mesh? Was she dreaming? Cold and uncomfortable, Ally tried to stretch out her aching limbs, but she couldn't.

Last thing Ally remembered was crossing the parking lot with her dry cleaning, then nothing. Blackness. Now, she was in some tightly enclosed space. In a panic, she tried to move but realized that her arms and legs were bound together, hog-tied; her secured hands brushed against the cold cement wall. Captive. Eric must have grabbed her! No, it couldn't be Eric! He was incarcerated.

Who had imprisoned her? Ally's heart rate accelerated, and her breathing became heavy and labored. Spots of light sputtered above, illuminating her submerged cell! She could make out the rectangular shape of heavy-metal, mesh lid with a ½ inch diameter rusted pipe that ran diagonally across the top forming a handle. Her four by three foot cell was about three feet deep. Her captor must be holding her in some kind of industrial, storage container.

It had to be Eric! He must have escaped. Flashes of light appeared overhead again, Eric must be moving around the grounds above with a flashlight. … Hadn't she foreseen this danger? Just this morning, she sensed it; the inevitability of her impending death. Now, she had no apprehension or fear just calm acceptance of her circumstances. Ally knew she was about to die.

As if in slow motion, Ally heard Eric's approach; he was coming to get her. Ally was determined not to beg or cry; she wasn't going to give him that ultimate satisfaction. She squinted, looking up as Eric

135

removed the lid of the cell. He reached down with a hunting knife and cut the line that held her bound hands and feet together, stowing the knife beneath his belt. Then, he roughly pulled her out to the adjacent ground above. Ally could not straighten out her bent limbs. Saying nothing, Eric painfully yanked her legs straight down. He mounted her, his back towards her face, pulling out a knife to cut the roped restraints of her feet. Ally felt a stinging gash in her leg through the uncirculated numbness of her limbs.

Morrison reversed his mounted position on top and faced Ally, looking into her eyes. He displayed the 7-inch hunting knife for her view, watching and waiting for her reaction. Ally tried to remain unresponsive as Eric drew the knife to the top of her neck, skirting the jawline. Eric pressed the sharp, steel blade against her exposed skin. Ally flinched as she felt the warm, trickle of blood on her cold flesh.

Then, he leaned in and paused, his face resting adjacent to her own. In a harsh, guttural whisper, he said, "I can't get carried away yet. For years, I've been planning and waiting for this day. It won't be quick; I want this kill to last a long, long time."

When Ally failed to react, Eric responded, "Then it's your daughter's turn." Ally jerked involuntarily, letting out an audible cry.

She felt his thighs tauten against her own, and the heat of his arousal sickened her already queasy stomach. Wrenching. No, no she couldn't heave, trying not to gag as she turned her head sideways, away from his disgusting utterances. Nearby, she saw the large corrugated, metal pipes. A water culvert? She wondered incongruously. A hysterical thought; did it honestly matter?

Eric placed his hands around her throat, turning her head to face him. He applied pressure. Ally kept her eyes tightly closed, trying to ignore the increasing pressure that correlated with the growing darkness. The guttural whispering continued, barely forming meaning through the empty void. "Your nude, dismembered body will be disseminated for all to see. And your decapitated head will be placed at that asshole, Bryant's front door! It's all your fault, you know. You should've kept your fucking nose out of my business. Now, you're going to pay for it. Your death will make a statement -you shouldn't have fucked with me!"

He dismounted her, shoving Ally over face first into the ground, reaching down and hoisting her up by the bonded ties at her wrist. He pushed her forward. Still woozy, Ally shakily staggered and stumbled forward on her weak, trembling legs; not wanting to fall forward, face first, onto the ground. With no way to break the momentum, she cringed at the perceived pain and damage that such a fall would inflict. The sluggish march continued for several minutes.

Ally stumbled, with hands bound at the wrist, she couldn't catch herself. She managed to stop her fall by jetting out her front leg in a lunge. Root instinct on her part, Ally shifted her weight to her back leg as she grabbed and twisted Eric's unprotected groin. Eric buckled forward with a screaming whelp of pain. Ally fell forward, her grip on Eric's private parts broke her damaging downward plunge. The flashlight flew out of his hand, smashing and breaking on the ground in the distance. Its light was extinguished.

Eric remained doubled over, clutching his mid-section while groaning in pain. Ally struggled awkwardly twisting her legs and body to obtain a standing position. Rapidly scanning the area, she clumsily surged into the blackened abyss of a rounded tunnel that was under construction. Ally had no hope for survival, but death from dehydration or starvation was preferable to the fate that Eric planned for her. She could choose the nature of her demise. She wouldn't be subjected to the degradation and spectacle of Eric's venomous malice.

Ally was confident that Eric would not pursue her into this underground cavern since his flashlight was destroyed in their struggle. She did not know how much time had elapsed, it seemed like ages since she had broken free from Eric. She continued to move in slow motion. Ally became alert to lights moving towards her from behind in the darkened passage. These lights were gaining ground on her within the limited scope of the narrow channel. Was Eric determined to run her down? He couldn't miss; the interior of this tunnel couldn't be larger than 10 feet wide. Ally continued to trudge forward unable to run, but she knew it was useless because he would soon catch up anyway. Her lifespan had shortened to a matter of minutes. It would surely be a more merciful death than if left to natural causes. With this thought, Ally turned to face her death; head on.

Oncoming headlights, mercifully but temporarily blinded her from this perilous predicament. Suddenly, five headlights, like glowing orb eyes, illuminated the dark surroundings. ...Oh God Almighty! What in the hell, is that thing? A machine? It was coming towards her! The rumbling mechanical litany of the charge, fueled Ally's adrenaline-filled senses, yet she stood rigidly rooted to the spot. Her breath was suspended. She was unable to breathe as her heart pounded in a deep, rapid beat. She was swiftly plunged into the deepest, darkest realm of abject terror; held in frozen immobility by the vision before her.

The orb-like eyes highlighted the moving mechanical parts of this freakish 'monster' machine, as a smoky halo of exhaust fumes outlined its hideous form. The greasy vapors preceded the unnatural beast and lingered in the still air. A huge metal arm reached out to strike her down with a multitude of sharp, shark-like teeth which brandished both hands of this alien contraption. While, the feet of this mechanical creature resembled two giant ninja stars with five cutting blades rotating in a circular motion, churning with effort, ready to cut into her vulnerable flesh. The image of this menacing fiend was similar to a giant mechanical scorpion in a sci-fi movie. The creature continued to advance towards her slowly as it filled the void of this interior cavern. –Nowhere to run or hide from it! There was no way to evade the emanating doom or the finality of her pending destruction.

Now, Ally ran as fast as she physically could, waiting for the final impact. Holding her breath, she pressed against the solid, dirt wall ahead of her; the tunnel passage had ended. Ally was at a dead end! Earth was crumbling around her as the rock and ground were being devoured by the arm of this gruesome machine. Ally tried to dodge away from the falling earth as she was being buried in the rubble that surrounded her. Ally covered her face. The darkness eclipsed and swallowed her up into a vast void.

That must be Morrison! What in the hell is he doing? Neal arrived at the Hemsdale Water project site, with his backup deputies five minutes behind him. He'd just seen the trespasser entering the unfinished tunnel in the cab of a 'road header' tunnel excavation machine. The interior of the tunnel was rough because it hadn't been reinforced with concrete slabs or stabilized in any manner yet. There would be no reason for him to enter the tunnel with the roadheader except...Holy Hell! He must have abducted Ally. Neil formulated that she must have escaped and run into this underground tunnel passageway.

Neal pursued the suspect into the subterranean corridor. He shouted through the intercom for the offender to stop because he was under arrest. Neal drew up on the tail end of the road header. He could see flaying arms in front of the machine.

"Stop or I'll shoot!" Neal shouted again through the intercom, over the noise of the machine. The man continued to his onward charge toward the desperate figure.

Neal fired twice at the operator of the machine; the man slumped forward, as the road header started eating into the earthen wall of the chamber. Ally? She was caught in the cascading rock and dirt.

Neal stopped his vehicle. He rapidly climbed into the cab of the road header and carefully, checked for the pulse in the suspect. No pulse. He pulled up the head of the man. Yes, it was Eric Morrison! Neal turned off the power switch of the excavating machine but left the lights ablaze.

Neal swiftly made his way around the front of the road header, digging through the rubble. He found Ally's head! Neal gently pulled up her head, while carefully supporting the neck until her upper torso was clear of the rubble. He felt a faint pulse at the base of her red, swollen neck.

"Quick, quick! She's got a pulse. She needs medical attention. The machine operator is already dead." Neal shouted out to the approaching deputies.

The deputies cleared a pathway for the Paramedics and dislodged Ally's legs from the debris. The medical technicians proceeded to place a neck brace on Ally and belted her down to a backboard before placing her on the gurney. She was still unresponsive.

"Wait, wait, I'm losing her. Quick, get the defibulator." The EMT shouted on the way to the ambulance. "No pulse, she's dead."

CHAPTER 9

In an elongated, deep tunnel, Ally looked ahead at the warm, glowing light. She happily moved towards its brightness. This luminosity radiated a feeling of intense security, comforted protection, and physical well-being. Yet, Ally heard soft whimpering in the darkness of this corridor. She looked around for the source of the noise.

A young boy sat butressed against the wall of this passageway. His arms tightly held his trembling knees, while his head slumped downward. He looked up at Ally with hollow eyes; it was as if she could see through him.

"You were supposed to survive. I wanted to make you understand. I tried to save you! Now, what am I going to do? I don't want to be stuck here forever. Please can you go back; you have to help me," the boy pleaded.

Ally recalled the vision with the large cats. Hadn't her unseen companion told her something about the boy's detached spirit? Yes; and now that spirit had to be reunified with the soul, in order to be made whole again. But how?   Wait, his final pronouncement had been that 'she needed to save herself, and reassert life.'

Oh God! The boy had just told her that she was supposed to survive. Ally was confused as questions filled her mind..   Did that mean she was dying? Or was she already dead? Had Ally failed her mission by focusing with such intensity on her death rather than on her own survival during those final minutes? She had just conceptualized these thoughts with the full implication of her death, when she experienced an unsurpressable tug, drawing her forward again.

Ally felt the persuasive pull of the glowing nucleus. As she was lured by the enticement of this beautiful light; Ally was also gently propelled frontward. She felt the expansive upsurge of incredible warmth, love, energy, and knowledge; eminating and filling her being as she drew increasingly closer to the epicenter. She zealously moved toward the light, eager to see and experience what lay onward in the center.

As Ally drew ever closer, she could see multitudes of 'beings' emanating various radiances of light, which seemed to correlate with the volume of joy, each being' experienced. Ally felt that she illuminated light as well and that she was part of their light. They were a part of hers! Feeling the essence of each being as she glided forward, even deeper into the core. She acknowledged and embraced her old friend, Jennie. Others exerted and enfolded her in their presence: her grandmother, David's Mom, and the soul of Bree.

Ally hadn't reached the heart of this incredible light; when Bree reached out and took ahold of Ally's hand, stopping her progression. Ally could feel the same ambiance of Bree, as before; and yet, she exuded an ageless, timeless aura, overflowing with wisdom.

Bree patted her hand and said softly, "Ally, you cannot continue on this journey."

"I want to see what's over there," Ally said eagerly, straining toward the luminated hub. It was essential that she reached this final destination.

"I know," Bree conceded gently with a nod. "But, it isn't your time yet."

"I don't want to go back! It's so amazingly beautiful here," Ally was overcome with dismay.

"I do, understand. You will be able to come back later and finish your journey." Bree smoothed Ally with wise reassurance, acknowledging Ally's sadness.

"Guess what?" Bree asserted now like her younger self.

"What?" Ally intoned; still, looking longingly ahead at the incredible nucleus of loving energy.

"You met Eric's spirit in the tunnel," Bree informed.

Ally nodded, "Yes, I don't completely understand why his spirit is there within the tunnel.."

"The spirit of Eric split off and died away; estranged from his soul when he intentionally planned and executed my murder. His earthbound soul is now just an empty vessel; a depository for dark forces," Bree said seriously.

"I'm beginning to understand," Ally said uncertainly.

"You're confused," Bree said with a sigh. "A disconnected spirit has only an essence of energy and cannot travel far from its root source of energy or its soul. Only a 'spiritualized soul' can make this journey into the light, since the path requires comprehensive vitality. Eric's spirit cannot advance into this realm without an accompanying soul. He's stuck, right where he is at, within the tunnel; unable to make any advancement towards the light."

"Okay," Ally asked hesitantly. "How was Eric's spirit able to communicate with me?"

"Remember I told you that a disconnected spirit carries a dimunitive amount of energy. His spiritual energy was absorbed into the quartz rock of the mine tunnel at the time of my death. Quartz is a good conductor of energy. His 'held' spirit attached itself to you when you came to find my body within the mine." Ally absorbed this knowledge.

"What does Eric want from me?" Ally questioned.

"Redemption. Eric needs to resurrect the wholeness of his being by reuniting his spirit with his soul. He has been trying to achieve his redemption, through you, since that juncture in the mine."

"How does my involvement affect this redemption process?" Ally inquired steadfastly.

"Eric's disconnected spirit has tried to make amends for his past deeds and prevent any further atrocities from his blighted soul. He has imparted information to you in order to stop any further damage to himself. In this effort, his lost spirit attached itself to you. If your complete soul moves onward into the spiritual realm, then

Eric's damaged soul will be left behind, beyond the reach of his spirit. Eric's disconnected spirit understands what his desecrated soul cannot.

The spirit of Eric had to ensure your survival; in order to allow Eric's disconnected spirit to re-enter his blackened soul. Once this redemption happens, his spiritualized soul can begin the first step on his intricate journey towards the light. However, Eric's path towards the light will be slow and tedious; since the radiance of his personal light is extremely dim due to his many transgressions. Moreover, it will take extensive growth and progress for Eric's impaired soul to truly understand and acknowledge the damage he wrought. "

"I understand," Ally said in repulsion, as she recalled all of Eric's nefarious transgressions.

"His soul will have to fully comprehend and accept the responsibility for his destructive deeds before he is finally allowed to enter the light. Until that time, you need to help him Ally like you helped me," Bree responded delicately.

"Yes," Ally affirmed as she visualized the scared, pleading boy within the tunnel. "

"You do, understand! See you later, Alligator," Bree said in enthused merriment just like the younger ambiance of her spirit.

"After a while, Crocodile." Ally felt a force pulling her back into the pathway, away from the beautiful and enticing light.

Ally came to an abrupt stop, somewhere in the tunnel. She attempted to trudge back down the corridor, but she was held stiffly in place. Ally looked around, unsure of how to proceed.

The hazy apparition of a beautiful young woman formulated itself, in front of Ally. The ghostly spirit struggled to fully manifest and communicate; as if the image was coming in and out of reception, frequently losing its signal. The femine form beseeched Ally for help in a halting manner "While earthbound, I lived in the same street as you, but I was murdered. No one is aware of this crime. Please disclose the truth; expose the Killer. *The apparition disclosed as she slowly faded off. She had dissipated, as quickly as she came.*

Ally was mobile again, moving back along the pathway. She then was looming above her own, injuried, body within the ambulance. She laid down on top of her body; she was infused back into life.

Neil followed behind the ambulance in his squad car. Silently, he begged for Ally, to be alright. One of the EMTs, from the preceding ambulance, radioed Neil. We've got a pulse; we were able to revive her.

"Thank God!" Neil said with a heavy rush of relief. "I'll see you at the hospital," Neil radioed dispatch giving his pending his ETA (estimated time of arrival) at Tri-County Memorial.

Klay finished helping Elizabeth unpack. Soon, she was properly moved into her dorm room at Acacia College. Then, they headed over to Klay's apartment to watch the episode of 'Mystery Source.' Elizabeth was glad that Klay's roommates were out because she didn't want to answer any questions about her sister.

Elizabeth fidgeted nervously throughout the broadcast. Afterward, she paced restlessly across the room unable to calm down.

"I wonder if your Dad's office has received any calls on Tabitha yet?" Elizabeth asked apprehensively.

"There's one way to find out. I'll give Dad a call." Klay headed over to the phone.

"Hi Mom, is Dad home? What? I can't believe it! I'll call him later." Klay looked troubled; his face lost all its color as he hung up the phone.

"What's going on, Klay?" Elizabeth said tensely.

"Eric Morrison abducted and attacked that Sullivan woman. She's in bad shape; they are in the process of transporting her to the hospital. Morrison was shot and killed at the scene."

"Damn it! Klay, I feel bad for that woman. But if she dies, I may never find out what she knows about Tabitha. Please Klay, could you take me to the hospital. I have to try and speak to her."

"Alright," Klay said anxiously, grabbing his keys.

Ally was barely conscious, but she was having another vision:

Ally was under the palpable blackness of the night sky —not a star could penetrate the oily canvas overhead. The darkness covered the Earth below, securing it, protecting the hunted. She heard a truck pull off the side of the road and a door open.

"That fucking cop finally quit tailing me. The fucking pig!" The harsh, male voice bellowed into the night from the area near the truck. "You're lucky; I can't take the time!" Ally heard something hit the ground and a ruffling sound. The door shut again, and the vehicle peeled away.

A thin cloud ebbed through the tarish night, skirting the blackened sky with a thin veil of muted, hazy light which temporarily highlighting the diminutive figure of a young girl. The lone child stood up and fixed her vacant gaze beyond, walking onward. The sight of a garbage can next to a picnic table seemed to penetrate the girl's consciousness. The child rummaged through the trash can in search of any edible food. Ally called out, "Is that you? Tabitha, it's Tabitha!

The EMTs rushed Ally in, on the gurney, through the emergency room doors.

"My sister —where is she?" Elizabeth demanded. She had

heard Ally call out to Tabitha and rushed over to the gurney.

"Whoa, hold up!" The security guard grabbed hold and held Elizabeth back. The medical personnel continued to work on Ally as they transported her back into an operating room.

"Klay, she knows where Tabitha is! If she dies, I may never find my sister," Elizabeth stifled a sob. Klay put his arm around Elizabeth's shoulder, gently pulling her into an embrace, rubbing her back.

"I've got to stay here at the hospital; in case, she comes around. I need to talk to her!"

"Yes, I know. I'll stay here with you. I'll give Marion a call and see if you can spend the night at her house." Elizabeth stubbornly shook her head at the suggestion.

"Elizabeth, you are not going to be able to see her past visiting hours. I honestly don't think she is going to regain consciousness tonight; she is going into surgery."

Again, Elizabeth had to admit that Klay was right. It was implausible that she would get a chance to talk with the Sullivan woman tonight. Remaining here in this waiting room would be a useless gesture, as well as a miserable waste of time!

"Okay, I see your point. I'll spend the night at Marion's house, because I'm going to be back here, first thing tomorrow morning." Elizabeth rejoined in persistent determination.

Elizabeth awoke; she was lying on her side. She glanced up at the familiar bedroom; she was back in the guest room of Marion's house. She hadn't spent the night in her dorm room yet. Elizabeth sighed; this room felt safe and comfortable; as long as she had 'her own' sleeping bag.

Elizabeth patted the well-established feel of her sleeping bag.

147

Even through spending every night in a sleeping bag wasn't customary, Elizabeth detested laying within anyone else's bedding. As a kid, she'd had enough of waking up in strange accommodations within unfamiliar surroundings. Sadly, wherever she laid her sleeping bag now, somehow felt safe and comfortable, because she'd never had a proper home. Would she ever truly feel grounded?

Elizabeth turned over, her eyes directed towards the ceiling above. "What the Hell! " Elizabeth opened her eyes wider; then rubbed her eyes vigorously to clear her vision. Then, she opened her eyes again. That Sullivan woman was hovering over her bed. The looming woman held out her hand towards her.

"No way am I going to take your fucking hand! Are you crazy?" Elizabeth asserted, glaring intensely as the Sullivan woman zoomed away, fading into a small spot.

"What the hell was that twisted dream about?" Elizabeth questioned resentfully; the dream scared her! It had been too visibly real. Elizabeth was born and bred into a harsh reality. Her upbringing had made her aware, alert to any pending danger. Consequently, this vigilance had always kept her safe. Thank God, she didn't have her head stuck in the fucking clouds. She couldn't afford the luxury of daydreams.

Elizabeth arrived at the hospital first thing in the morning. A small group of people clung together, their grief evident. A family member must be here in the emergency room, Elizabeth surmised. A doctor entered the waiting room.

"Mr. Sullivan, may I speak to you?" Elizabeth's head shot up as the realization, set in.

Oh God, she prayed that the Sullivan woman was okay. She moved near the doorway in order to overhear the doctor's conversation.

"Mr. Sullivan, your wife flat-lined during the surgery; we temporarily lost her. Thankfully, we were able to revive her. I believe she's reached the turning point and is beginning to stabilize. But, we want to keep her in the hospital for a few days as a precaution," the doctor confided.

"Can I go in and see her," David Sullivan asked huskily.

"In about an hour, she still coming down from the anesthesia."

"Thank you," David went over to the rest of the family to give them the update.

Elizabeth thought of that twisted dream she had last night. That Sullivan woman flat-lined! No, there was no connection. She was over-tired and imagining things.

Ally was at the entrance to the tunnel. She felt herself propelled rapidly towards the light again. For a moment or was it an eternity, she bathed in the beautiful light, looking down at vibrant vistas of indescribably beautiful scenery. Ally recognizes the girl below. It's Elizabeth! She floats down to the girl, sleeping in the bed. Ally smiles when Elizabeth sees her. Ally reaches out her hand because she wants to show the poor child that her sister is still earthbound. Give her hope! But, Elizabeth pulls away. Then, Ally feels a strong force drawing her back through the tunnel. Until, she sees her body lying upon the operating table.

"We've got a heartbeat," Ally hears hollowly from a distance.

She is floating somewhere near the ceiling. Then Ally is drawn back towards her body which is lying dormant on the table.

Despite the heavy medication, Ally laid in abject misery in the hospital bed. Her whole body hurt; unlike, the pain-free existence she experienced while within the tunnel. Ally had pleaded with her family, to go home and get some rest, which allowed her to do likewise.

Ally didn't want her loved ones, her family, to see her current despondency. She hated the fact that she was back here; Earthbound. She was afraid that each of her loved ones would feel rejected and would be wounded, emotionally, if they were aware of her true feelings.

However, Ally managed to give her mother, Rene, a mischievous wink, "Just wait Mom until I tell you about my journey."

"Ally, you don't mean..."

"Yes, I do! But, you'll have to wait for all the details," Ally said managing a weak grin. "I want to do justice in the telling."

Ally laid back; her eyes closed. Images and feelings from her time in the tunnel flooded her mind. Ally didn't think about these images or feelings; she re-experienced them in vivid detail.

Elizabeth approached the hospital bed with determination. She eyed the woman lying on the bed. Was she asleep? No, she saw the woman scratch her arm.

"Mrs. Sullivan ...Ally, please you have to tell me all that you know about my sister. You said she was alive when they brought you into the hospital." Ally slowly opened her eyes to find a frantic young woman; Elizabeth Lenard. The girl's eyes were wild with apprehension. Ally wanted desperately to alleviate this girl's fears, lighten her load, despite her weaken condition.

"Elizabeth, I understand that it is difficult for you to accept what I'm going to tell you. But, I'm going to lay out the information I've received from my 'visions' since our first meeting. I'll give you all the information I've received. It's the best that I can do," Ally said haltingly.

"Okay?" Elizabeth said defensively.

"And PLEASE, don't give me attitude! I'm not up to the task,"

Ally said bluntly, beyond the polite amenities. Elizabeth looked startled; taken aback.

"I'm sorry. I ...I realize you're not feeling well. I appreciate that you're willing to talk to me," Elizabeth faltered.

"When I spoke to you in my yard; I had received a heinous vision. I believe Eric Morrison abducted Tabitha from your aunt." Ally jumped in immediately, trying to maintain her energy reserve in order to finish this conversation.

"Yes?"

"He was flustered because Tabitha's reactions were atypical. She seemed to be in a dissassociative state. Do you understand that term?"

"Yes, my sister didn't speak. And Tabitha seemed unresponsive to what went on around her," Elizabeth said in surprise; Ally nodded.

"Eric took your sister to his trailer. That's when he took the photo."

Elizabeth nodded, her eyes fearful.

"Two police officers came to the trailer and started asking questions. Tabitha was only several feet away at the time. After they had left, Eric unraveled. He planned to kill Tabitha and dump her body over the stateline in Oregon," Ally continued weakly.

Elizabeth looked distressed. Quietly, she questioned, "After he freaked out, did he kill her?"

"No. But, I don't know where to find your sister or what happened to her after that night." Ally's voice trailed off. Talking had enervated Ally; she fell silent in fatigue.

"Please...how do you know?" Elizabeth encouraged Ally to continue; trying to curb her mounting impatience.

"I had another vision last night when they brought me into the hospital. I heard a man stop his truck. I'm sure it was Eric. He was ranting because a police officer had been following him. He also said that he couldn't take any time. He dumped something onto the ground and then, took off." Ally faltered before she weakly pressed on.

"Following the tail lights and noise, I went into the clearing. I saw Tabitha get up in that burned out forest clearing. She was walking through the area. Then, she rummaged through the garbage can. She was alive. That is all I know, I swear it!" Ally closed her eyes; drained and exhausted. She didn't know if she could continue.

"She's right you know." Both Ally and Elizabeth were startled and looked towards the sound of newcomer's voice. A teenager had entered the room.

"Sheriff Bryant said I might find you here," she said, looking directly at Elizabeth. The girl continued to stare affectionately at Elizabeth as if she were the only person in the room.

"It's been a long time, but I'd recognize you anywhere," the girl replied tenderly.

The teen had golden brown hair and blue-grey eyes. But, she bore a striking resemblance to Elizabeth. Ally shifted her gaze from the newcomer to Elizabeth. She saw the color ebb from Elizabeth's face as the shock registered in her eyes. Elizabeth stood in frozen bewilderment, silent; the teenager returned her stare without comment.

"Tabitha. Tabitha, is that really you?" And Elizabeth burst into tears. Tabitha rushed over and embraced her distraught sister. The two girls had clung together in an all encompassing embrace for several moments before any more words were spoken.

"Yes, I'm here, " Tabitha said gently. She broke the embrace by lovingly placing her hands on Elizabeth's shoulders; in order to gaze into her sister's face.

"You-you- you can talk!" Elizabeth exclaimed.

"Yes, I can. I found my voice."

"Oh God, Tabitha! I thought I'd lost you. It's been so long. ...I can't believe you're here! Oh God; I've missed you." Elizabeth rambled almost incoherently.

"It's okay. I'm here, now," Tabitha reassured.

Ally, revitalized by this touching reunion, sat up in bed. She wiped the flow of emotional tears from her eyes that continued to stream down her face.

A little while later, Tabitha sat holding Elizabeth's hand at Ally's bedside.

"So, you're a psychic, Ally?"

"Yes, I am," Ally said looking steadfastly into Elizabeth's eyes. Elizabeth dropped her gaze downward; looking uncomfortable, embarrassed.

"I heard what you told Elizabeth. My memory of that night was clouded. I could only remember bits and pieces. What you said, helped me fill in the gaps."

"What happened to you, Tabitha, after that night?" Ally asked; Elizabeth's head shot up, looking inquisitively at her sister.

"Let's see, my personal recollection of events is rather sketchy" Tabitha formulated her story. "In late September 1992, a couple of hunters found me foraging for food in the trash bins at a campground. I don't know how many days I was out there in the woods. These men took me to the hospital."

Tabitha continued brokenly as if she was retrieving this material from various sources. Most of this information must have been reported back to Tabitha from official reports.

"I arrived at the hospital, extremely dirty, cold, and hungry. I was admitted. I couldn't speak, so the doctors performed several exams to determine if I had a traumic brain injury or something. Nothing seemed to be physically wrong with me. So, the doctors and nurses started calling me, "Grace" because it was by the grace of God that I survived." Tabitha smiled half-heartedly, "I must have been in bad shape when I came in."

"It's a good thing that Morrison is dead. Or I'd kill the Creep myself!" Elizabeth said fiercely; Tabitha placed her other hand comfortingly on top of their clasped hands.

"It's alright, Elizabeth. It's all over now."

Tabitha continued her story, "I, 'Grace' was subsequently placed in a psychiatric treatment center. One of her nurses, Sara, wanted to assume guardianship of me. She loved and cared for me. Sara pulled all kinds of strings and went through much red tape to pursue the guardianship. In fact, she almost had to quit her job to make the guardianship happen."

"Sara would've pursued adoption. But, we didn't know what my personal circumstances were at the time. Sara didn't think it would be fair to my biological family, who may have been lost in the wildfire. She figured that I might have extended family out there, in the world, that couldn't find me."

"Sounds like a wonderful person," Ally commented.

"Yes, she is," Tabitha said with a smile.

Tabitha continued: About a year and a half after I was rescued from the woods, I was sitting with Sara watching TV. . I saw a young girl with long dark hair, and I called out, "Elizabeth!" Sara nearly fell out of her seat but quickly recovered.

"Oh Tabitha," Elizabeth said softly, her eyes filled with tears.

Sara asked me, "Who is Elizabeth, honey?'"

I told her, "She's my sister!"

Sara asked me my name. I told her, "I'm Tabitha, not Tabby because Elizabeth told everyone that I wasn't no cat." Tabitha said with a chuckle as Elizabeth grinned.

Sara asked me who I lived with before I was found in the

woods. I told her, "everyone."

Then Sara asked me where I had lived. I told her, "everywhere."

"The only definite answer that I seemed able to give her was that I had a sister named, Elizabeth. I couldn't even explain how I came to be in the woods."

Elizabeth opened her mouth to speak but seemed unable to utter any words.

"Sara's friend saw the *'Mystery Source'* program and recorded it. When Sara saw the show, I was sleeping over at a friend's house. Sara called me and told me to come home. There was something important that I needed to see. First thing I saw was my sister, Elizabeth," Tabitha said cheerfully. Elizabeth was crying again. She attempted to shield the tears from view by holding her hand up to her face.

"I should go and give Sara a call. Let her know what's going on." She held out her hand to Ally. "Thank you for all you did; I really appreciate it." Elizabeth looked awkwardly at Tabitha; uncertain, about what she should do now. She was at a loss. Incredibly, she was still speechless!

Tabitha looked at Elizabeth and laughed, "Elizabeth, please come with me. I need to introduce you to Sara. Man, I don't ever remember you being so quiet!"

Elizabeth burst into laughter, "Excuse me! I'm not quiet!"

EPILOGUE

It was over three months since her death. The subsequent resuscitation infused her daily life with greater depth and significance. She no longer overlooked the simple pleasures and the happiness of small moments. Ally was also aware that there was an interconnectiveness between all living matter as well as, other people. She didn't selfishly guard her time and energy anymore.

Initially, when Ally returned to her present life, she was overwhelmed by a bout of depression. Her journey beyond into the spiritual realm was magnificent, filled with vibrant beauty and ever-enduring love. The positive energy of the light was abundantly full of wisdom, kindness, compassion. Any positive emotion that one could name and even those wonderful feelings that defy description. It had been an incredible journey; something too exquisite to behold.

However, Ally knew that her destiny here in this life wasn't completed and that she had a higher purpose for her existence. It gave her -hopeful enthusiasm. And she certainly couldn't fear death, anymore. Ally only hoped her life, as well as her death, brought about beneficial results for the living as well as the spirits involved.

Ally often thought of that ghostly young woman who approached her in the tunnel. She had asked around, posed some inquiries. But, Ally didn't have a name or a time period to frame her investigative efforts. Intuitively, she knew this female spirit would find a way to reach out and communicate with her when the time was right. When this contact was made, Ally would help this delicate woman in any way she could.

Last month, Elizabeth came to visit her. She came to apologize for her past behavior, as well as, to express her gratitude. Her feelings were sincere! Even though, the poor girl stumbled all over herself, and the words got caught in her throat in expressing the sentiment.

During their visit, Ally cheekily admonished Elizabeth. She told the young woman that when someone offered her their hand, it was only polite to take it. Ally had held the girl's gaze; she saw the color ebb from Elizabeth face as her eyes widened. Yes, Elizabeth recalled that image of Ally hovering over her bed that night. Ally then held out her hand. Ally had enjoyed 'funning' the girl a little bit.

Elizabeth told Ally that Tabitha returned to Oregon; in order to finish her senior year in high school. Elizabeth promised to visit Tabitha over the Christmas holiday, and meet her guardian, Sara. In addition, Tabitha promised to link up with Elizabeth after her graduation. Her sister also was considering enrolling in Acacia College, next year.

Overall, Elizabeth's life was on the upswing. She was still dating Klay, and both were in school, doing well. Ally wouldn't be surprised if they eventually married. Recently, Ally asked Neil about his feelings regarding their developing relationship between his son and Elizabeth. Neil told Ally that Elizabeth was 'one tough, little cookie!" But, Neil reluctantly admitted he liked the girl; now that she wasn't up in his face all the time.

"Geez, can you believe it?" Neil had told Ally. "Elizabeth still thinks Morrison was terrified of her because she would've 'taken him on.' That girl truly believes that she's invincible!" Neil said dismissively, but Ally wasn't so sure that Eric hadn't been intimidated.

Despite the differences in the socio-economic status between Eric Morrison and Elizabeth, their upbringings and personalities bore many similarities. Yet, Elizabeth chose to become her sister's champion and protector; this role seemed to both frighten and repel Eric at the same time; a blatant reminder of what he could have been to Caitlyn, to Tammy, to Shilo.

It was still incredible to think about! Eric had been the fifth victim. Somehow, when this truth emerged, Ally felt she had always intrinsically known the answer. Perhaps at the time, she'd simply been in denial, refusing to accept this answer. Her anger, hate, and disgust for the man had been too overpowering.

Nonetheless, Ally had learned a major life lesson from an unlikely source; Eric. Love and hate aren't truly opposing emotions as many believe. Generally, hate grows out of one's ability to be hurt by another; the fear of being hurt by another person causing you pain. Eric's overwhelming fear and pain had steadily grown into his all-encompassing hate. Ironically, Ally had heard that the spirit is attuned to the divine; whereas, soul is more grounded in earthly concerns. Yet, even Eric's spirit seemed to operate from a basis of fear. From the beginning, Eric had used either agonizing nightmares or moralist tales to enlist Ally's help. Whereas, Bree always operated from a place of love. The heavenly dreams came from Bree, along with all her endearing compassion.

Ally conjectured about what had happened to Eric in the paranormal realm; inspired knowledge that Ally was sure originated from either Eric or Bree. Eric's disconnected spirit couldn't reunite with his damaged soul until after Eric's death. Therefore, his spirit had latched onto Ally in order to make amends and improve the quality of his afterlife. This youthful spirit tried to warn her about the pending danger from his adult self. In part, for his own self-protection. When Ally died, Eric's spirit was carried into the tunnel with her. But, his disconnected spirit couldn't move any further because it was still tethered to his damaged soul; its life force. If Ally had moved fully into the light, then Eric's spirit couldn't return and reunite with his earthbound soul.

Ally caught sight of a butterfly, watching its erratic flight. Odd, she thought, it was far too late in the year for butterflies. Then, she heard the soft voice of a young boy whisper in her ear. "The butterfly is the symbol of the soul, representing new life after death. A true icon of spiritual transformation! Thanks," the voice faded away as the butterfly flew off into the distance.

ABOUT THE AUTHOR

This is Casey Jo Jukes' second novel, a sequel to '**Animas Within**.' A third novel, '**Injured Sparrow**,' is in the works. She has an extensive work history as a social worker and counselor in various social welfare programs. She currently lives in Northern Nevada with her husband, and has two grown children.